# Surrender to Love

## Denise R. Williams

Oasis Publishing

This book is a work of fiction. Names, characters, places and events are products of the author's imagination and have no relation to anyone bearing the same name or anyone who has experienced similar circumstances. All incidents are pure invention. Any semblance to actual events, locations or persons, living or dead, is entirely coincidental.

Copyright © 2007 by Denise R. Williams

All rights reserved. The reproduction, transmission or utilization of this work in whole or in part in any form by any electronic, mechanical or other means, now known or hereafter invented, including photocopying and recording, or in any information storage or retrieval system, is forbidden without written permission, except for the use of short quotations or occasional page copying for personal, group or reviewer use. For permission contact: Oasis Publishing Group, 3506 Hwy 6, Sugar Land, Texas 77478.

ISBN:   978-0-9797689-1-0
        0-9797689-1-8

For information regarding special discounts for bulk purchases, please contact Oasis Publishing Group at (281) 778-9782 or oasispublishing@entouch.net

*Thanks for your support*
*Denise R. Williams*

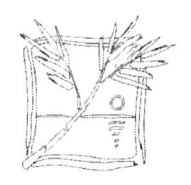

# Surrender to Love

## Denise R. Williams

*For my children, Maya Marie and Anthony James,
the inspiration for all that I do.
When I grow up,
I want to be like the two of you.*

# Chapter 1 – Maya

I stepped out of the shower and wrapped a towel around the naturally wavy hair my two best friends, Lillian and Donna, never missed an opportunity to tell me I was so lucky to have.

"Girl, you got that *good* hair," they would say as they ran their fingers through it. My girlfriends were not the only ones to share that sentiment. On more than one occasion I'd had black women who were total strangers ask where I'd purchased it or what process I'd used to achieve it. When I informed them it was natural, some asked if they could touch it. I was never sure if it was because they doubted my veracity or they were simply amazed at the possibility. I shrugged off their comments, though it always felt a little disconcerting, especially when they came from Donna, the most socially-conscious-down-with-the-people-sister girl I knew. She was the last person from whose lips I would have expected to hear the words "good hair." What? Other people's hair robbed banks and molested little children?

Whatever. We all had our issues and Lillian and Donna were my girls. In fact, they were the only people with whom I kicked it on a regular basis and even our hanging out time had lessoned considerably over the past six months. Me, because I was re-focused on my career after breaking up with my boyfriend, Deuce, for the third and final time; Lillian because she was consumed by the demands of mothering twin one-year old boys who were my God sons; and Donna because she was going through a nasty divorce with her husband of almost twenty years and eating her way through every restaurant in Chicago.

But anytime you threw three black women together it's inevitable hair will become a topic of conversation. Maybe India Arie could sing herself into believing *she* was not her hair, but most sisters still had a ways to go on that journey.

I loved the funky hair style Lillian wore. I was actually a little envious that even if my hair was that short, it would never look that good, but she, too, told me she wished she had *my* hair. Of course, the remark usually coincided with her hair appointment with her so-so chic hair stylist, Gustave. He was my stylist, too, but I felt I couldn't really claim him since I only saw him twice a year for a trim and deep conditioner.

Truth be told, I would go bald before I dished out the kind of cash Lillian threw down; three hundred dollars *every* six weeks for a relaxer and trim plus weekly style appointments that averaged almost a hundred, and don't mention color!

Not that I couldn't afford it if I wanted to. I had the money. I had met my goal of earning three times my age. I was thirty-three-years-old and made a hundred thousand dollars before bonus. I just couldn't shake my mother's tutelage on the importance of frugality. I still marveled that a woman who never made more than twenty thousand dollars a year was able to send me to one of the finest colleges in the country and I graduated without a nickel in financial aid to pay back. Well, thank goodness for my mother's ability to pinch a penny and that she taught the skill to me. And an even bigger thank you that I had the kind of hair I only had to run a little styling gel through and it automatically fell into a soft mane of curls. Otherwise, unlike my girl, Lillian, my head would be looking a mess.

"Watch the pennies and the dollars will take care of themselves." That's what my mother always told me. And I took her advice to heart. I wasn't cheap. I certainly wasn't one of those people who excused herself and went to the bathroom every time the check came. I ponied up when it was my turn to pay. And I spent money, lots of it. One look in my closet proved that point. Just my shoe collection was worth a small fortune.

No, I wasn't a penny pincher like my mother. I just made sure I spent money wisely. I only bought quality, upscale, designer stuff but I couldn't remember the last time I paid full price for anything. I didn't need to. And neither did anyone else if they had taste and knew fashion. An outfit from TJ Max or Loehmans could look as good as one from Saks or Nordstroms.

Now my girl Lillian? The philosophy with which she grew up was another story. We were neighbors, from fifth grade until we graduated from high school, both of us were the only children of single mothers. But her mother and my mother were about as different as night is from day. And not just because my mother's complexion was about a shade darker than milk chocolate while Lillian's mom could have passed if she wanted to. That is, until she opened her mouth. From the moment she started talking there was no doubt Lillian's mom was straight-up southside Chicago hood.

"Got to pay to play," was one of her favorite expressions. Of course, she always added, "Goddamn it" on the end. The other one was, "Use what you got to get what you want." Her mother used to tell me that all the time. "Girl, with that hair and that ass you could get you a professional athlete like that," she would say as she snapped her fingers. "Get you some green contacts and shit." She'd let the sentence trail off as if the vastness of my potential bounty was too great for her to articulate. Of course, she never talked like that around my mother who would have gone ape-shit if she'd heard Mrs. Turner dishing up that type of counsel. My mother valued brains, not physical beauty. Whenever someone complemented me, my mother's standard reply was, "She's twice as smart as she is pretty."

Not to say Lillian wasn't smart. She'd graduated from the University of Illinois with a degree in Business and worked in finance at a big downtown Chicago firm until she got married two years ago. It's just that climbing the corporate ladder wasn't her focus. Finding a *man* who was climbing the corporate ladder was. And Lord knows girlfriend worked it. I never saw her when she didn't look like she was headed to a fashion shoot even when she was just going to the grocery store to pick up formula for the twins.

"I may be out of the work force but my husband ain't. I'm not going to let one of those little skanky hoes turn his head. He needs to know that what he's got at home is better than any shit he can get at the office."

Amen, sister. Like I said, Lillian was no dummy. She was smart enough to know men like her husband, Rick Smythe, were one in a million. You could pretty easily find tall, dark and handsome. But tall, dark and handsome making two hundred thousand dollars a year was about as difficult as picking the winning combination of digits for the Super Lotto. And tall, dark and handsome making two hundred gees who wanted a *black* woman was like winning the Powerball. Girlfriend had used what she had to get what she wanted.

Caramel brown and petite, Lillian reminded me of Jada Pinkett-Smith before Mrs. Smith started sporting the long hair. Though girlfriend was only five-four people assumed she and I were the same height because she was never, and I mean never, caught in public without four-inch heels, even when she was pregnant. And for the past three months she wore a spiked hairdo that added another inch to her frame. Gustave, our stylist, was expensive as hell but he put his foot up in some hair. You had to give my man his props.

And Donna? She reminded me of Angela Davis. We'd hit it off when she joined Narcisco Industries, the company for whom I'd worked since graduating from college, to head up Quality and Regulatory Affairs. She was cool and always kept it real. I really admired her down-with-the-people attitude coupled with her ability to figure out the power structure and use that knowledge to work the system. My girl didn't brag but she had an undergraduate degree from Spellman *and* a law degree from Harvard. She knew her stuff and anyone who spent more than five minutes talking to her knew she knew it, too. She was a sister not to be played with.

Donna had sought me out in her first week on the job to pledge solidarity in "a-sistah's-right-to-wear-her-hair natural" campaign. I vowed allegiance even though we both knew it was a lot easier for me to wear my hair without benefit of chemical alteration than it was for her. My *natural* looked like the perms our white female co-workers spent big bucks trying to emulate while Donna's *natural* made her look like a Rastafarian.

"What's the big deal with black people and hair?"

"Only bitches with hair like yours ask that question," she shot back.

She put me in my place quick. She knew that I knew

what the big deal was. It wasn't as though I wasn't used to the attention my hair caused. Even back in the day, every Sunday while I waited in the church vestibule while my mother changed from her choir robe, someone couldn't resist asking me, "How does a girl dark as you get such good hair?"

"Well, look at this dark girl now," I said to the bathroom mirror. I stared at my reflection and liked what I saw. Since I had gotten over Deuce, for real this time, not just the lip service I had given myself the other two times we split up, I felt reborn. Not reborn in the way promised by television evangelists when one accepted Jesus Christ, but reborn in the way of a caterpillar who awakens as a butterfly; reborn in the way of an ugly duckling who becomes a swan.

Forty-eight hours ago I started the day as a successful mid-level human resources executive at one of the companies the *Wall Street Journal* had named in its "Five to Watch" column and ended the day with a promotion to Vice President of Human Resources reporting directly to, James Caplin, the man touted to be the next chief executive officer for the entire corporation.

Yes, life was good. I was back on track for the life my mother and I had envisioned for me. For us, actually. I blinked back the tears that popped into my eyes when I thought about my mother. Even though we never had the kind of relationship I always wanted, I missed her. She and I were never cool the way Lillian and her mom were. I didn't go to her for advice on men. We didn't chit-chat multiple times a day. We didn't go shopping or share leisurely afternoons at the spa. I would have paid for it. But she refused my offers of assistance.

At first I thought it was pride but I eventually figured out she just didn't like that kind of thing. Massages and facials were too frivolous for her. And I didn't enjoy myself when I forced her to do those girlfriend kinds of things because that look on her face like she'd sucked on a lemon would start pissing me off. But still I wished she was here with me. I couldn't exactly explain it. Since she died I felt like a socket with nothing into which I could plug myself. I felt disconnected, ungrounded.

"Stop it," I said out loud as I strapped on my high heeled sandals and willed myself not to think of anything except the celebration Lillian had planned for me. Tonight was a night to party, not a night to think about my mother's death or my boyfriend's betrayal. Asshole.

I hoped my mother knew her baby-girl had done good, had made her proud. Surely, she knew that I was livin' la vida loca.

"Can't nothing stop you but you," my mother had repeated like a mantra for as long as I could remember. "You got the smarts to do anything you set your mind to as long as you don't get caught up in some mess."

By mess I knew she meant man-relationship-drama. Her relationship with my father had been less than idyllic. I knew that, not because she talked about it, but because she refused to discuss him at all. Never. Not a word. If I didn't know better I would have assumed my conception had been immaculate.

When I was a little girl I used to ask her if my daddy had died and she told me that I never had a daddy. Which in reality I guess I didn't. Sperm donor does not a daddy make.

Once our Cousin Lottie, who was like an aunt to me, slipped up and mentioned his first name. Sonny. I was never sure if that was his given name or a nickname. "Goddamn it, don't that girl look just like Sonny?" Lottie had said to my mother as she stared at my photograph that my mother kept on her bedroom dresser. They didn't realize I was hiding under the bed. I liked it under there. It was quiet and dark. Not scary dark. Movie theater dark. Dark but non-threatening.

My mother's response had been, "I don't remember what the no good nigger looked like."

When I stuck my head from under the bed and asked Cousin Lottie if she knew where my daddy was, my mother told me, "M.Y.O.B." Mind your own business. "Stay out of grown folks' conversation."

I was too young to articulate that *my* father was *my* business. So that was it. That's the only time I ever heard him mentioned. Oh well. Life goes on. Even after death. Life continued. And my boyfriend's departure was a welcomed relief. I had side-stepped a potential faux-paus from which I would have never recovered.

If we had stayed together no way I would have been given this chance. No. Not given. I had earned this promotion. I was the one who worked seventy hours a week and still completed the executive MBA program at the University Chicago, one of the top business schools in the nation. I was the one who delivered whatever was expected of me all the time, every time. This vice president's position had my name on it. I knew it. I had known it for a while. And I was pleased the executive staff of Narcisco Industries had finally acknowledged they knew it, too. Me, daughter of a single unwed mother from Jericho, Alabama. Ghetto girl made good. Me, Maya Marie Latimer, Vice President of Human Resources for a Fortune 100 corporation.

I turned on the stereo and sang along with the tune kicking from my top-of-the-line Bose speakers. The jersey knit fabric hugged my curves like a race driver on a test track as my hips swayed with the music. Thank goodness, so far, I didn't have to work at keeping my flat belly. I hated to see women in clingy clothes with bulges sticking out everywhere. My mother and I had won the genetics lotto in that regard. Latimer women carried our weight in the butt not belly. And thanks to Beyonce and J Lo, butts were big. No pun intended.

I took one last look in the mirror, fluffed my hair, grabbed a jacket just in case the Windy City lived up to its reputation and shut the door of my half a million dollar condo. It only had one bedroom but when I lounged in bed I enjoyed a view of Lake Michigan. And when I sat in my living room the lights from Chicago's ritziest neighborhood shimmered below — the Gold Coast, home of the Magnificent Mile and some of the Midwest's most fabulous people, including me.

## Chapter 2 – Maya

As I drove up, the five-bedroom, two-story brick colonial home of my girl, Lillian, rose like a fortress against the night sky in the northern suburban community of Winnetka, Illinois. Though Peaceful Acres subdivision had advertised one acre lots, Lillian made sure to inform me the Smythe-family estate actually occupied almost one and a half acres and exceeded the village's median home value of seven hundred fifty thousand dollars by almost a quarter of a million.

But the house, illuminated in the soft glow of an outdoor lighting package that cost more than my first car, reminded me of a mausoleum. I never mentioned that little detail to Mrs. Lillian Turner-Smythe—Smythe spelled with a "y" and an "e" not an "i" simply ending with an "h". I wondered if Rick's family had changed their name like Jewish parents who gave their children two names, one Hebrew to be used in religious ceremonies and another more gentile derivation for use with the outside world. If he were *Smith* instead of *Smythe* would he have still made senior vice president before his thirtieth birthday?

Though I loved Ms. Lillian, she was a pretentious bitch, not the type of person who took criticism well so I knew better than to say anything. And the house *was* beautiful. It was the type of home one saw in the pages of magazines like *Architectural Digest*. And though as little colored girls growing up on the southside of Chicago we knew people lived in houses like these, we never imagined people who looked like us lived there. No doubt, as a race, we were making progress. At least some of us were. I was. Donna was. Lillian and Rick definitely were. Their boys would grow up knowing black people could live large even when they didn't play ball or sling drugs.

But I grew up secure in that knowledge, too. I didn't have a lot of material possessions as a kid but I never felt poor. I always knew if I worked hard there was nothing that could be denied me; at least not material things. Though I worked at it, the only subject I couldn't seem to figure out was the relationship thing. Unlocking the secret of how to acquire stuff was easy; how to find someone to love and make them love me back was a lot trickier.

I walked up the brick pavers that led to the patio of Lillian and Rick's house.

"The masons who made these have been in the brick making business for three generations," Lillian informed me the first time I'd come over to see the house. "In a few years you won't be able to get hand made bricks anymore."

I could tell from the way her lips twisted, as if she'd drank curdled milk, that I should be incensed at the notion of mass brick production. Though I didn't say it out loud I thought that there was no way in hell I would have spent the money they spent importing bricks from South Carolina. If I could have bought them from the clearance section at Walmart, I would have.

"We just don't have that kind of history in our community," Rick chimed in. "What? Our kids are going to say their granddaddy passed a liquor store or a beauty shop down to their daddy and now it's theirs? Most of our kids don't even know who their daddies are."

At the time I made no comment, but maybe lingering memories of that conversation was what gave me the creeps about this place. It let me know I still had a ways to go in my transformation from Eliza Doolittle to Princess Di.

I had erased all traces of ethnicity from my speech pattern. I was positive colleagues who hadn't met me face-to-face couldn't determine over the phone that I was black. I learned to play golf, even developed a decent game. I didn't want to be left out of the information loop at company outings because no one wanted to pick me for their foursome. I took tennis lessons. At that I was actually pretty good. I even tried skiing but had to draw the line there. It was too damned cold on the slopes. Though I hated the sport, I still owned all the best accoutrements. I could sky-bunny in the lodge around the fire with the best of them. Yes, I had filled in most of the gaps from my lower class upbringing but attributed my lack of interest in the Smythe-family driveway as a neglected crack that still needed mortar.

But what could you expect? I grew up without a driveway at all which actually, was not a problem since my mother never owned a car which was still not a problem because my mother never learned to drive. Until we moved to the "house" as we always referenced it, we lived in an assortment of apartment buildings, all in a four-block radius of Martin Luther King Drive. My mother had to stay on the number seven bus line. That route took her directly to the suburb where she worked for two different white families, cooking and cleaning. Any other bus line would have required her to ride downtown then transfer adding almost an hour to her daily commute.

So when one of the husbands of the families for whom she worked pulled some strings and got her a job with the city, and we moved off the number seven line, I felt like we'd hit the lottery. She rented a brick bungalow next to Lillian and her mom, with two bedrooms and a small back yard. When I graduated from high school my mom moved into an efficiency apartment in a high rise building downtown where she didn't need to ride the bus at all. She was able to walk to work until she got sick and was forced to go on medical leave.

But tonight, me and my girls were gathered under the stars on a patio that boasted an outdoor cook area more expansive than most people's interior kitchen. We raised our flutes brimming with Kristal, the only champagne worth drinking according to our hostess, in salute of my latest career achievement.

"Did you see the article that ranked Narcisco as the best medical device company in the world?" Donna asked.

Lillian's eyebrows arched in disapproval as Donna, the only one of us whose dress size was double-digit, only a ten, but double-digit never-the-less, popped another shrimp puff in her mouth. Donna stared directly at Lillian and stuffed in two more appetizers.

"What did you make them for?" Donna started the sentence then stopped to correct herself. "What did you *buy* them for, if not for us to eat and enjoy?"

Lillian rolled her eyes. "If I don't say it, who else will?" She didn't back down. Lillian returned Donna's stare. "Every time I see you your ass has gotten bigger."

"What you doing looking at my ass?" Donna stuffed another shrimp puff into her mouth. "Besides, I didn't have lunch today." She sucked the crumbs off her fingers. "I lost my appetite after reading all that bullshit about what a great place Narcisco is to work."

"They've been good to me." My words slurred together. I held up my glass in silent salute to my employer. It had been awhile since I had consumed anything alcoholic. I was buzzing.

Lillian lowered her voice and spoke to Donna in her best mommy tone. "Honey, how much weight have you gained since the separation?"

"No, she didn't," joked Donna. She waved her hand in front of her face, snapped her fingers and moved her neck and shoulders back-and-forth in mock exaggeration of a round-the-way girl.

"Fifteen?" Lillian lowered her voice to just above a whisper, "Twenty?"

"Leave her alone." I came to Donna's defense. If eating brought her a little comfort, so what?

"Thank you." Donna stood up on legs that were shaky from alcohol consumption and reached for the bottle. She refilled our glasses. "Everybody's not going to be a size four."

"Size two, thank you very much," said Lillian. She twirled around in front of us. Her four-inch heels clicked on the brick pavers. She was in better shape than before she'd had the babies. Like I said, girlfriend was no dummy.

"Are those Manolo's?" I asked.

Lillin plopped down in the overstuffed lounge chair and held up her foot. Donna and I examined the sling back pumps with admiration. They were fabulous.

"An extravagance from my days before children."

"That was your choice." I extended my own well-muscled leg for the women to see the stiletto-heeled sandals I wore. "Children over Jimmy Choo. Me? I'll take the shoes every time."

Our laughter rippled across the patio like waves in

the kidney-shaped pool that took up a third of the backyard. And Lillian said it was a total money pit. She didn't even know how to swim and Rick was rarely home long enough to enjoy a dip in the pool though he had been on his college swim team.

"Girl, you should see the body on this man," Lillian had bragged after she slept with him for the first time. "I've never seen someone so slim with such well-defined muscles."

"You sure he ain't on the down-low?" Donna had asked. "You never know about brothers these days."

"Shut up." Lillian tried to laugh Donna's comment off but I was glad she'd opened the door. I had wondered the same thing about the brother. Since our book club read the E. Lynn Harris trilogy, *Invisible Life*, *Just as I am* and *Abide with Me*, we all looked at men a little more closely, especially if they veered outside the traditional black man norm of manliness. A black man with a body like a dancer did set the alarm bells to ringing. And with almost seventy percent of new AIDS victims being black women, sisters needed to step up their due diligence when it came to understanding the sexual appetite of the brothers with whom they were sleeping.

But Rick's credentials made Lillian put her apprehensions aside and give him serious consideration. She assured us she was being careful. Good for her. Everybody needed to be treated as if they were innocent until proven guilty. But I know that I would have passed on Rick and bee lined it to someone like my ex, Deuce. Which was even worse judgment. That's why Lillian was married with two kids while I was still dating and breaking up with men like I was in high school.

I understood why Donna was stressing over the notion of being single again. Girlfriend had never even had an AIDS test. I'd had three. But when she got married right after college graduation there was herpes but even that wasn't really top of mind. And I don't think she'd been with anyone except Bradley. From the day they started dating, now even while they were separated, she'd never had sex with another man. The thought of not being married scared the shit out of her. I empathized. Dating wasn't all that it was cracked up to be.

I told Donna everything would work out for her just like it all worked out for our girl, Lillian, because I didn't have the heart to tell her what I really thought; that if she and Bradley got divorced she better be prepared to spend the rest of her life alone. Hopefully, that wouldn't happen to her. But she needed to be prepared for the possibility.

Congratulations to Lillian for finding herself a man to marry. "He's the kind of man women long for and men wish they had the balls to be," she had told us one night in a drunken diatribe on the virtues of Rick. So on Lillian and Rick's wedding day when me, Donna and ten of her other closest friends stood up and watched her pledge her life and love to the man of her dreams she had beaten the odds half the other single African-American women out there hadn't been able to overcome. She became a married woman.

Lillian refilled my glass. "I'm so proud of you, Ms. Vice President of Human Resources."

I shrugged but I couldn't stop grinning. This promotion took me from the cogs of middle management to the upper echelon of senior executive. Not only was I the only woman to join the corporate executive team, I was the only African-American. You go girl. And the public relations department was working overtime. *Black Enterprise* magazine had already contacted me. They planned to feature me in an upcoming issue on "Power Brokers in Corporate America." God, I wish my mother was around to see that, especially if I got the cover and the folks in PR thought there was a good chance that I would. I had the look. And the magazine had been courting Narcisco to become a major sponsor of a black women's health initiative they were kicking off.

"That's right! Go on with your bad self," added Donna.

"Please." I waved away my friend's compliments.

"What is this? Your fifth promotion?" asked Donna.

"Seventh, but who's counting?" I had collected my two hundred dollars, passed go and was working my way around the game board.

Lillian placed grilled salmon on the top of the chopped salads she had prepared. She poured the last of the champagne into her own glass. "Rick would have shit bricks if I had started making the kind of money you're making."

"Well thank God I don't have a Rick to worry about."

Lillian shrugged and nibbled around the edges of a lettuce leaf. "You don't mean that."

"The hell I don't."

"Every woman in the world ain't looking for a Rick, you know?" I said.

"Yes they are. If the right guy came along you'd be married by night fall."

Donna grunted and stuffed more salmon in her mouth.

"It's not what you're eating," quoted Lillian to Donna. "It's what's eating you. You can't eat your way to happiness."

"But I could be eaten to it."

We laughed. Leave it to Donna to keep it real.

"Nasty, heifer," said Lillian. After a few seconds she added, "I wish I could get some of that, too, though."

"What? I thought Rick was Mr. Lover-man?"

Lillian leaned toward Donna. "Girl, why doesn't anybody tell you once you get married the sex dries up like a raisin?"

"'Cause it ain't supposed to."

"Everything I've read talks about how babies and sex don't go together. Well, at least not after you've made them."

"Don't you know you can't believe everything you read?" Donna asked me. "That's your problem. Always trying to figure shit out from the sidelines."

Lillian put down her fork. "Things didn't change between you and Bradley?"

Donna shook her head. "Not in the beginning. Not for a while, actually."

I could see Lillian's wheels turning as she thought about what Donna had said.

"You think Rick's messing around?" Donna asked.

"I don't know. I don't think so."

"The wife never does."

I rolled my eyes at Donna. We both knew Lillian could take a grain of sand and turn it into a beach.

"The boys are in bed before eight. We have the time. Rick's either not around or not in the mood." Lillian stood and smoothed the fabric of her outfit over her hips. "It's not me, is it? I still look good, right?"

"Sit your skinny ass down. Hell no it's not you. It's them. Remember that, it's always them."

Lillian smiled. "You're right, girlfriend. It must be him because I'm fabulous."

"Notice who made no comment." Donna tilted her head toward me.

"What?" I asked.

"You know what."

"I am minding my own business, enjoying the delicious meal my friend has prepared with her very own hands."

"Ain't she a bitch?" asked Donna. She pointed a fork full of salmon toward me. "Since you and Deuce broke up, how many guys have you been out with?"

"You're not my mother." I snapped my fingers and shook my head from side-to-side. "And even if you were, I'm a grown-ass woman. Have been for a good while now, thank you very much." Actually, I hadn't been out with anyone. Men were the last thing on my mind. Until I figured out what I was doing wrong, I wanted to keep a low profile. I had bought about twenty different books on relationship dynamics and was reading my way through them.

"I haven't had a date since my separation and this heifer has probably been beating men off with a stick."

Lillian stared open mouthed at me. "You've been holding out on me?"

"How did I become the focal point of this conversation?"

"Because you're the only one gettin' some," replied Donna.

"Says who?"

"I just hope you're being careful."

"Abstinence," I said, "the ultimate act of carefulness."

"You don't have to play Miss Hard with us." Lillian sipped her champagne. "Everybody wants someone with whom they can share their life."

"And the mortgage payment." Donna winked at me.

"I did not marry Rick for his money."

"And Clinton didn't have sex with that woman."

"Shut up. I didn't. I love Rick."

Donna shrugged. "Did I mention any names?" She looked at me. Using an accent as if she were in an old English play, she said, "Methinks the lady doth protest too much."

I grinned and looked at Lillian. "Why are you getting so defensive? Nobody said you did. We know you love him."

"And even if you did marry Rick for his money, good for you," Donna said. "I'm so sick of these poor-ass-no-bank-account-having-brothers I could puke."

"Wait a minute," I piped in. "When I say that type of thing you give me a lecture on how the power structure in America keeps black men down."

Donna waved a carrot stick at me. "Well, now that I've had the opportunity to talk to a few of them I've revised my hypothesis. Most of these brothers are suffering from a low self-esteem victim mentality and they need to grow the fuck up." Donna slapped my extended hand a high-five. "Can I say it?"

"Say it, sister." I had no idea what was about to come out of her mouth but I wanted to hear it.

"I'd rather *her* marry Rick for his money," she said tilting her head toward Lillian, "than some white bitch getting him."

"Shut up," Lillian pouted. "Both of you. I didn't marry him for his money."

"I ain't saying that's what you did but if you did, more power to you."

Lillian and Donna grew silent, each lost in her own thoughts.

"Forget these men," I said. "I'm on sabbatical."

Lillian pushed back her plate, the food half eaten, and stared intently at me. "I don't blame you, girlfriend. Dating had started to wear me out."

"Well, you did treat it like your second full time job."

She shrugged. "You have to work for the things you want. You think you're going to be successful just leaving romance to chance?" Lillian looked at Donna for several seconds then turned her gaze back to me, but not before Donna understood her meaning.

"Fuck you. We were happy for a good ten years."

"But you've been married almost twenty," I reminded her.

"You didn't have to marry the first man you fucked, you know?" Lillian said. "But I know your generation is a little more old-fashioned in that regard." Lillian liked teasing Donna that she was approaching forty.

Donna chuckled. "Or in your case the twentieth or was it the thirtieth?"

"Ouch." I chuckled. "Ladies, we have a tied score."

"Besides, he was the second man I fucked, thank you very much."

Lillian pushed her food around her plate. "You don't

leave your career to chance. I wasn't going to manage my love-life like that either. Marriage is the biggest, most important *investment* you can make."

"Don't say that." I looked up into the night sky filled with stars. "Marriage is about love and commitment." I really believed that. Probably another reason I wasn't married. I knew that real-life romance would never be like Romeo and Juliet, who even wanted that kind of intensity, anyway. But I wasn't ready to accept that it couldn't be like Jack Nicholson and Helen Hunt in *As Good as It Gets*. Like Melvin, Jack's character, I believed that my significant other should feel that I made him want to be a better person. And that's what I wanted from him. I wanted him to complete me. But that was a different movie.

"Aw, ain't that sweet."

"Come on, I thought you were on my side." I looked at Donna for support.

She shrugged. "My name's Bennett, I ain't in it 'cause I think marriage is whatever two consenting adults determine they want it to be."

Lillian turned her attention back to me and asked the question I had asked myself a thousand times, though I had never been able to truthfully answer it.

"Aren't you ready to settle down?"

Like a little kid, I put my fingers in my ears and hummed loudly, "La, la, la, la, la, la." I didn't want to think about love and marriage. If I thought about it I'd feel compelled to do something. And I hadn't figured out what I needed to do to make it happen.

Lillian's voice rose higher to be heard over my gibberish and Donna's laughter. "Your ass ain't getting any younger you know?"

"She's like a fine wine," Donna said. "She's growing in bouquet and flavor." I wasn't sure if Donna was defending or mocking me.

"That turns to vinegar if you wait too long to drink

it," Lillian added.

I picked through the remains of the salad that Lillian served on the sterling silver platter I had given them as a wedding gift.

"Who do you think you're talking to?"

"What?"

The ranch dressing that dripped off the stalk of broccoli I used as a pointer was the only indication that Lillian had struck a nerve. Normally, I never wasted calories on condiments like sauces and dips. If I'm going to consume calories from fat, give me a slice of sweet potato pie.

"Seriously, what are you talking about?" repeated Lillian.

"You're the one who's never got anything good to say about Rick since you guys got married."

"That's not true."

"After you worked him like Ali worked George Foreman to get him to the altar I might add," said Donna.

"From the moment you got back from the honeymoon you've been complaining about the man."

"Amen," said Donna.

"You lying bitches."

"He works all the time ..."

"You never have sex any more."

"He treats you like a second class citizen."

We giggled like school girls. Even Lillian. She knew we spoke the truth. She held up her arms in mock surrender, "All right, all right, maybe I have had a complaint or two but marriage is an adjustment, especially when you have kids right away."

"No thank you." I placed my hand over the top of my glass in refusal of the refill Lillian offered. "Where's the joy in getting your heart broken all the time?"

Donna patted my hand. "Deuce was an asshole."

"Now you tell me." I finished the last sip of champagne. I was ready to go home. I felt weepy. I was drunk.

"I ain't one to say I told you so but we told you that nigger was an asshole from the very beginning."

Lillian nodded in agreement.

"Besides, you can't trust those short mother-fuckers. How tall is his ass? Four feet eight?"

I laughed. "A little taller than that."

"Not by much," added Lillian.

"Short men always have something they're trying to prove."

"Here she goes," I said.

"Forget you, I know what I'm talking about."

"Napoleon complex," Lillian said.

"It doesn't matter how much money they make or how powerful their position, they ain't happy until they're making you unhappy."

"But your soon-to-be-ex is six foot three."

Donna grunted. "Well, his ass is just a plain fool. Height has nothing to do with his issues."

We laughed.

Donna took the last shrimp puff from the platter. "We had our share of good times, though. I can't blame him for being what I knew he was. Even in high school I knew his ass loved money."

"Get a little, then get the hell out." I spoke my new philosophy out loud for the first time. "Men have been doing the shit for centuries." Before I got involved in another real relationship I was going to take the advice of one of the authors whose name I didn't even remember but her philosophy resonated with me. I was going to do some trial runs. The author was right. You don't run the Boston Marathon without doing a few 5K races first. "Experiment. Go out for just the fun of it. Have sex just for the pleasure of it. Don't attach so much meaning to every encounter."

"All right, there now." Donna held her hand up in the air and wiggled her fingers. I reciprocated by wiggling my fingers against hers.

"I'm glad I don't believe you really mean that, otherwise I'd have to find someone else to be godmother to my babies."

Donna looked at me as though she were appalled. "You whore," she said to me.

We burst out laughing. Between the three of us, Donna was the most open-minded and least judgmental.

"I know I like to complain but I also know that shit is a part of life." Lillian filled her glass with the remains from the third bottle of champagne. "Where's the joy in having all the stuff in the world if you don't have anyone to share it with?"

"Speak for yourself. I have someone to share my life with."

Lillian's head popped up like a jack-in-box, "Who?"

I motioned for my friends to stand up. When we were all on our feet I opened my arms like Moses parting the Red Sea. We fell into one another's arms in a group hug. "I have my girls. Who needs a man?"

"You do," said Donna, "if you're looking for anything more than this hug."

# Chapter 3 – Tony

The countertop of a small kitchen that hadn't been updated since the seventies was piled high with dirty dishes. The browned remains of a macaroni and cheese casserole, candied yams, and chicken and dressing hugged the sides of the dishes in which they had been baked like drowning people clinging to life rafts. Brenda scooped the greens and salt pork swimming in the large pot that still simmered on the stove into a plastic container.

"You know mama would have wanted to save the pot liquor."

"And momma would kick my behind if she saw me letting my eight month pregnant baby sister wash all these dishes. Sit your butt down." I pulled Brenda from the sink and nudged her toward a hard-backed kitchen chair. "Sit," I commanded.

While my sister took after our mother, short, light brown skin, with a propensity to get hippy, I took after my father. I had only seen a picture of him. My mother kept it in a shoe box with lots of other old pictures under her bed. He wore a sailor's uniform and she had on a tight red dress and knee-high boots. He had been, maybe still was, the epitome of tall, dark and handsome. I had never met him. I doubted that he even knew I existed.

"You don't be telling me what to do," she said. "You ain't my daddy."

Even as a kid she couldn't stand for anyone to tell her what to do. But this had been our dynamic for years, me acting more like a father than a brother. I was the one who threatened to kick the asses of the boys who chased her home from school, one of whom she later married and was her baby's daddy. It was me who wiped blood from her scraped knees when she fell down at the skating rink. Even before he died, her father was rarely around and our mother was exhausted from the demands of cleaning other people's houses. Before Brenda said anything else, Monica, my girlfriend for the past eight months, walked into the kitchen.

"Hey, honey-bunny, how's it going in here?"

I turned from the sink in time to see Brenda roll her eyes.

"Almost ready to go? You know I have an early meeting tomorrow."

I took three deep breaths before I responded. "Babe, I told you, you didn't have to come."

Even though the water was turned on full blast I heard Brenda sighing. I knew Monica heard her, too, but she didn't seem phased. In fact, she'd never let Brenda's less than warm reception bother her. She was always pleasant but never tried to suck up like some of the chicks I'd dated. It wasn't hard for women to figure out how important my family was to me. Monica got it. She understood. She just didn't buckle down to anyone. That was one of the qualities I really liked about her. I knew I could take her anywhere and she could handle herself.

"Of course I had to come."

"To keep her eye on you," Brenda mumbled underneath her breath. "Don't worry about me, big brother," Brenda said. She eased her swollen feet from the sturdy black shoes she'd worn all day. "Dean would never believe I'd wear some shit like this," she said, looking at her feet. "He used to tease me that I was living a secret life as a hooker. Fuck me shoes, he used to call them." Brenda bit her lower lip to stop it from trembling.

I squeezed her shoulder as she smiled in private reminiscence of Dean. Never in my wildest dreams would I have imagined my sister a widow. Even the word, widow, sounded too old fashioned and out of place to have any meaning in relation to her.

Ain't life a trip? Dean had escaped the perils facing young black men in major urban cities like Chicago to perish in a desert far from home. The army, the institution meant to be his salvation from the streets, had been betrayed him. No wonder people hated the government.

"Just because you're in the family way," said Monica from the doorway, "you don't have to sacrifice style."

Brenda stopped massaging her toes and looked at Monica who seemed oblivious to the message contained in Brenda's gaze that had narrowed to two little slits.

"One of the vice presidents at my company was always fly, shoes, suits, everything. In fact, I think she dressed better when she was pregnant than she did before or after she had the baby."

Maybe Monica didn't get it but I understood the look

on my little sister's face. It said, get that bitch out of here before I hurt her.

"Babe, why don't you go get our coats?"

Monica winked at Brenda before she headed to the front closet. I listened to the sound of her heels tapping in double time.

"She must be hell in bed because everywhere else she's a total bitch."

"Be nice. That could be your future sister-in-law." I took a stack of dirty dishes from the sink and dropped them into a large garbage bag.

"Hey," said Brenda.

"You don't need this crap."

Brenda opened her mouth to protest then changed her mind. "You're right. Throw the shit out."

Under different circumstances I would have teased her for giving in so easily. That never happened.

"Just tell me this," began Brenda.

I stopped and gave her my full attention.

"Why do you keep picking these power-hungry corporate babes? They ain't interested in having a relationship with anyone but themselves."

I sighed and resumed the chore of clearing the sink and countertop. "Come on, Brenda, I don't want to hear that lecture again. I know she rubs you the wrong way but Monica's cool. She's good people."

Like a flash flood that comes out of nowhere, tears welled up in Brenda's eyes. Her lower lip quivered. She waved away my look of concern. "Dean was good people and what did that get him?"

I was silent. She had me on that one.

"Only three more months and he was coming home for good."

I wrapped my arms around her. "I'm so sorry, baby-girl. We don't have any business in this war anyway."

"I told him not to join up. I told him."

"I know, I know." I held Brenda while her body

shuddered. I'd tried to talk Dean out of signing up, too, but I understood why he joined the military.

"Man, what's a brother to do?" he'd asked me. "Slinging? Working at Mickey Dee's?" I couldn't think of a better alternative either. With mediocre grades from an inner-city high school that was on academic probation more often than it was off, no money for college and no hope of any type of scholarship since the athletic and artistic programs had all been discontinued, there weren't many options available to a young brother. Even better than Brenda, I knew the temptations he'd resisted to become the man he was. And I had been proud to call him, not a brother-in-law, but a straight-up brother.

"Did I tell you the baby is a girl?"

She had told me that at least a dozen times. I simply nodded and said, "Yeah, you told me."

"Most guys want a son but Dean really wanted a little girl. Of course, he was going to spoil the shit out of her."

"Don't worry, her Uncle Tony will spoil her rotten."

Brenda wiped the tears from her eyes and nodded. "I know."

"I got my girls covered."

"Ready?" asked Monica. She had my navy blue cashmere coat draped over one arm, a gift she'd given me after she got a bonus that was two thousand dollars more than she had anticipated.

"I'll meet you at the car, okay?"

Monica nodded then said to Brenda, "I'm really sorry for your loss."

"Thanks," said Brenda without enthusiasm. I watched Brenda watch Monica walk out of the kitchen wearing a coat that cost more than a year's rent for the little house she and Dean had lived in since their marriage almost three years ago.

"Thank God that woman is out of my house before

her head starts spinning around. Lord knows I don't need to see that shit."

Even though Brenda didn't crack a smile, I chuckled. "So sue me for wanting a woman who doesn't need me for just a paycheck."

"What about choosing a woman who needs you for something, anything other than you know what?" Brenda pointed to the front of my pants.

I knocked her hand away and chuckled. "Stop being a slut."

"Me? You're the one living out these bitch's Mandingo fantasies."

I dried my hands on the dish towel. I didn't understand why it was so hard for Brenda to see my point of view. "Look, I don't want a woman who if something happens to me ends up like momma."

Brenda rolled her eyes. "I know you never forgave momma for not handling her business with my daddy."

I shook my head and stopped her. "Momma and Ernie's relationship was their business."

"You don't mean that."

"Yes, I do."

"Momma didn't know."

"All right," I said. "Momma didn't know."

Maybe Brenda believed that but I didn't. And if she didn't know, she should have. How could my mother live with a man for seven years and not know he was still legally married to another woman? Especially when they had a kid?

"She didn't know," Brenda said again.

"All right, she didn't know." So when Ernie died of massive heart failure it was his legal wife who benefited from his social security and got the pension from the plant where he'd worked for almost thirty years. It didn't matter that they hadn't been together for over a decade. She, not momma, was the one who had the piece of paper.

"Momma didn't have an issue doing day work. Besides, she got to take me with her."

I held up my hand in surrender. "I know. This ain't about momma and her decisions, okay?"

Brenda nodded. "Okay. Believe me, I ain't in the mood for an argument."

I smiled at my baby sister. She rubbed her eyes and looked just like she did when she was a little girl and the sand man was kicking her butt.

"I just want a woman who has something to show for her time on this planet. Is that so wrong?"

Brenda shook her head.

"To have a woman who ain't got to take no crap from a man, even me, just to make sure her kids have a roof over their heads and something to eat. I want a woman who can bring home the bacon if she needs to."

"Even if the bitch can't fry it up in a pan?"

I laughed. "Uh-oh, you sounded jut like momma. Always worried about a woman's cooking ability."

"Oh, God." Brenda laughed. "Next thing you know I'll be asking you to cut down the corn on my pinkie toe."

I looked at Brenda's feet. When I looked up, she burst out laughing. "I swear, you so damned simple."

I wrapped my arms around my baby sister and hugged her tightly. "You okay?"

She nodded.

"For real?"

"As okay as I can be, considering." She left the sentence unfinished but I knew what she meant. Considering she had lost the man she had loved since middle school; considering she was entering motherhood without a husband and her daughter would be raised without a father. She had become the one thing she'd promised herself she would never be, a single mom.

"What about you? Are you okay?" Brenda reached

up and patted me on the head, an old habit from when she was a little girl and I would ride her on my shoulders. She would tap my head to let me know that everything was all right up there.

"I'm fine."

"I know you are. That's why all these babes want to be on your jock."

I laughed. "Shut up. The women I date are too damned old to be dating somebody just because they want a good looking man on their arm."

"Whatever." Brenda looked like a windup toy losing momentum. "I just want you to find a woman who sees you for the wonderful person that you are."

"You and me both."

"I'm so glad I never had to go through all that drama. Ain't this dating shit wearing you out?"

I grunted as I gave the kitchen counter a final wipe down.

"Your ass ain't getting no younger, you know?"

"Men don't age. They grow more distinguished."

"Bullshit. You lose your hair and your dicks don't get hard."

Even though I knew Brenda was hurting she couldn't repress her sassy attitude. "Why you have to talk so nasty?"

"Sometimes the truth is nasty."

I knew she loved Dean with all her heart but I never worried about her being one of those women who would take too much crap from her man. She loved hard but she stood up for herself.

"Got to love you first." Our mother had told us that on more than one occasion after Ernie died. Maybe if someone had given her that advice before she hooked up with both our fathers things would have ended up differently for her.

I smiled at my baby sister. It would be tough but I knew she would make it. "Besides," I continued, "we may lose our hair but our dicks can get hard forever." I kissed her on top of her forehead. "Ever heard of Viagra?"

"Take two pills and call me in four hours. Is that how it's gonna be?"

"Don't worry, baby-girl. I hear you."

"Enough said then."

Brenda massaged her belly. "I guess I'm just being selfish. I want my baby-girl to have a few cousins to grow up with."

I winked at her. "Maybe Monica and I will work on that tonight."

"Oh, God, you trying to get me to go into labor?" Brenda leaned on the kitchen table for support.

"Be nice."

"Okay. For you."

"Sure you don't want me to help you clean up the rest of this mess?"

"I'm sure," said Brenda. I need something to keep me busy tomorrow. I know all this hasn't really hit me yet."

I nodded. "I'm here for you, you know that, right?"

She nodded.

"No matter how early or late."

"Love you, big brother."

"Love you, too."

# Chapter 4 – Tony

Monica pushed the key fob and immediately the Demon, as she called her jet black Mercedes, sprung into readiness. "Brenda okay?" She took my arm and stepped over the crack in the third stair. I made a mental note to come back later in the week with my tool box. I'd also noticed the hinge on one of the kitchen cabinets needed to be repaired.

Monica held my hand as we walked to the car whose seats would be warm by the time we got in. Whoever said money can't buy happiness never owned a Mercedes.

"God, I feel so bad for her."

I tried to detect the sarcasm Brenda always heard whenever Monica spoke but I couldn't. To me she sounded genuinely concerned. Maybe I was pussy-whipped. As I looked at Monica, I felt that familiar stirring in my groin. She was beautiful, five-foot seven inches, about one hundred fifty pounds, big enough to have a little meat on her bones but slim enough to be devoid of excess fat. And though I knew it sounded cliché, her breasts were like ripe melons. No matter how skilled the surgeon or how expensive the saline implants, as a breast connoisseur, I could tell, even before a woman took off her shirt whether they were real or fake. Monica's were real; just the way I liked them. I got an erection when I thought about how her boobs would swell even larger when she became the mother of the children I very much wanted to have.

But it wasn't her physical appearance that most endeared her to me. It was the way she maneuvered through life, disciplined but not conceited, friendly but with boundaries that were well defined and incapable of being breached, sexy but demure. She was the type of woman I could have brought home to meet my mother then take home and screw all night. The consummate woman; the appearance of a Sunday School teacher by day but when the lights went out, the sexual abandon of a whore.

"Hey." Monica reeled my attention back to her. "Is Brenda okay?"

"As okay as she can be under the circumstances."

Monica handed me the car keys and waited outside the passenger door. She always made me feel like I was the man in the relationship. And that she was glad about it.

"I don't know what's wrong with brothers today," she had complained one night when we lay in bed, spent and content after making love.

"Why are you thinking about other men when you're in bed with me? I must be losing my touch."

She chuckled and spooned closer to me. "You and I both know that's not true."

I smiled. Even though I was secure in my ability to please my woman it never hurt to hear confirmation.

"I was talking to my girlfriend, Beatrice, right before you came over."

Black women like Beatrice were the reason so many successful brothers said, "Screw it" and dated outside the race. While Beatrice was fine, nice boobs, juicy behind, she had a criteria list the size of Texas proclaiming what she wanted and expected from a man. The brother had to be all-that-and-a-big-bag-of-chips yet she was selfish, mean-spirited, one pancake away from being fat and only made a little over minimum wage working as an executive assistant.

"You know she went out with that guy she met in the elevator of our office building?"

"The stockbroker?"

Monica sat up and pulled the covers over her bare chest. I pulled the sheets back around her waist. "If I have to listen to a Beatrice story, you got to give me something."

If I wasn't afraid of losing it or having to kill another man for looking at it, I'd carry around a naked picture of her in my wallet. I guess I was pussy whipped.

"Well, he takes her to this beautiful restaurant, tells her to order whatever she wants."

"That was brave of him. It must have been a first date and he'd never seen that girl eat." She could put a bigger hurting on a slab of ribs than I could.

Monica narrowed her eyes. I raised my hands in surrender. "Sorry."

"Then when the bill comes he tells her to just leave the tip. He'll take care of the rest. And says it like he's really done something."

I shrugged. "Yeah?"

"You know, just because a sister makes her own money she still needs to be pampered and made to feel like she's special."

"So since she had to leave the tip she didn't feel

special anymore? The chick probably had lobster and filet mignon. Maybe he couldn't afford to leave the tip."

Though I always picked up the tab when Monica and I went out I understood all brothers couldn't afford to, at least not all the time, and at least not all the time with women who expected to go to five-star restaurants every time you took them out. Half of the time the sisters were making more money than the brothers anyway. Women wanted to have their cake and eat it too.

That's another thing I really liked about Monica. She never rubbed it in my face that she made more money than I did. And when we did something on her tab it was usually supplemented by her company. Nothing like dating an account executive with a generous expense account. Yeah boy.

Monica hugged me to her chest as we set in her car in front of Brenda's house. I rested my head on her shoulder and for the first time all day, relaxed.

"My honey-bunny's had a long day?"

I nodded. I had been at Brenda's house since five o'clock in the morning.

"Everything was perfect though. Your effort showed."

"Thanks." She always knew the right thing to say.

"Brenda's lucky to have you."

Monica squeezed my knee as I pulled out of the parking space. Though my Acura TL and I were still having a love affair, after driving Monica's car I felt like my baby rode like a pick up truck. Monica looked over at me. "No music? This is a first."

She had become quite a house head since I turned her on to house music when we first starting dating. A cat I worked with from Detroit hipped me to it almost ten years ago and I'd been a groupie ever since. In Chicago, house music was still an underground thing, but he had a regular Sunday night gig going at a club on the north side called Delano's. It became one of my favorite spots to hang out when I felt like just chillin'.

As if she didn't want to waken the people sleeping in the bungalows that whisked by as we drove, Monica spoke in a hushed tone. "So did you pick up the suit I had them holding for you at Macy's? I'm pretty sure I'm getting account manager of the year so there's going to be lots of picture taking."

Though the architecture was humble, the houses in this southside neighborhood marked the initial exodus of people to Chicago's out skirts. And almost eighty years after their original construction, though the families living inside them had grown darker and lost an Eastern European cadence when they spoke, they still represented hope and achievement for their residents.

"I love it that you have the physique to wear this season's trimmer cuts." Monica was a clothes horse, and I mean a Clydesdale, not a Shetland pony. My knowledge about fashion and designers had improved during our time together. I gave the girl credit. She had helped me take my look up a notch or two.

The steering wheel glided through my fingers as I turned a corner. I pulled onto sixty-third street, an avenue that in its hey day was to Chicago what Lennox Avenue was to Harlem during the Renaissance.

"It's way past time for you to retire this one." She turned her nose up, her face distorted into a grimace as if I'd farted in the car, when she looked at the navy blue pin-stripe suit I wore.

"What's wrong with this suit?" I had only had it on three or four times. I wasn't the suit type. Blue jeans, a French cuffed shirt and a pair of funky cuff links were more my style.

"Nothing's wrong with it."

I hated it when she used that I'm-about-to-tell-this-customer-something-they-don't-really-want-to-hear voice on me.

"It's just not as stylish as you deserve to be."

Last month I'd flown to New York and spent the weekend with her after she'd concluded a business trip. We spent over four hours in the Roberto Cavalli Fifth Avenue boutique looking for the perfect outfit for her to wear to the awards ceremony at her incentive trip. I remained silent and drove. The Demon was so quiet, if the car wasn't moving I wouldn't have known the engine was on. I knew looking good for that night was important to her, and on this trip I was an extension of her.

"So does that mean you didn't pick up the suit?"

I wasn't in the mood for an argument and I knew one was coming as soon as I answered her question. Stop being a wimp, I told myself. "No, babe, I didn't pick it up."

Monica nodded. She patted my knee. "You've had a lot going on. Are you going to be able to? I could probably swing by at lunch tomorrow but you really need to be there in case it's not perfect."

"Don't worry about it."

Monica was silent for several seconds. "Honey-bunny, the trip's next week. Are you sure you should cut it so close? What if ..."

"I'm not sure that I really need a new suit since I'm not going to be able to go anymore." There I'd finally said it.

I watched Monica out of the corner of my eye. She blinked twice, her head tilted to the side as if she needed to interpret what I'd said from English into her native language. "Not going to Jamaica?"

I noticed how the people hanging out on the corners stopped what they were doing and followed the progress of the Demon as it sliced through the night.

"What did you say?"

I didn't respond. She wasn't hard of hearing. She'd heard me. She just didn't like what I'd said.

"Come on, Monica, we just buried my brother-in-law. My sister is about to have her first baby, alone. You really think I'm going to leave her right now to fly off to your sales meeting?"

Monica took a deep breath. I knew that she was counting to ten. In all the time we'd been together, I'd never heard her raise her voice. Not even in bed. The girl had control.

"Yes, I expect you to go." From the modulation of her tone, someone who didn't know her would never suspect she was upset. But I could tell from the way she blinked she wasn't just upset; she was pissed.

"It's only three days and this trip has been planned for months. If, heaven forbid, something were to happen, which it probably won't, it's only a two hour flight back."

She exhaled. Blink, blink, blink, blink. "Yes, I expect you to go." She said the final sentence as though she were summarizing a presentation.

"Monica, this is family. She's my sister. You can understand that, right?"

She took another deep breath. This time she must have counted to twenty since it took her longer than usual to respond. "I understand your responsibility to family."

Keep your mouth shut. De-escalate conflict, I repeated over and over to myself. She had the right to be disappointed. I was disappointed, too. Who wouldn't love an all-expense paid trip to a five-star resort?

"I'm the oldest of six kids, remember?"

I nodded. I'd lost count of the number of times she had reminded me that she was the oldest of, not one baby sister, but three younger sisters and two younger brothers whom she practically raised while their mother and assorted fathers spent most of their childhood inebriated or buzzed or both.

"Honey-bunny, what about your responsibility to me?"

Okay, she changed strategy on me. Since logic wasn't working, she'd make an emotional appeal. I understood

*Surrender to Love*

why she was so successful. The babe was smooth.

"Shit happens, babe. Plans change; you can understand that, right?"

Monica stared out of the window.

"Mind if I turn on some music?"

She shrugged but didn't speak. When she did, she enunciated each word slowly and distinctly. "Cleary, supporting me doesn't mean shit to you."

I wasn't going to allow myself to be baited into that argument. "That's not true, Monica. You know how much you mean to me." I was flattered she was this upset about my backing out. After all, she would still be there with two hundred of her closest coworkers. I didn't think my going really meant that much.

"Tony, I mean this, okay?"

"Okay."

"Are you listening to me?"

"Yeah, babe, I'm listening." I turned down the volume of the CD I was listening to. The bass faded to the background like elevator music.

"If you can't go with me on this trip after all the arrangements have been made, after I've told all my coworkers that you're coming, I don't think our relationship has a future."

"Come on, Monica, let's not do this." I looked from the road to Monica. Her stoic countenance was reminiscent of an old world dime store wooden Indian. "I want to go home, get undressed and lie next to you. I just need to chill. Can you understand that? Can you do that for your man?"

Monica didn't look at me. She stared out of the window as we moved down the expressway toward the bright lights and tall buildings of downtown Chicago. It was so long before she spoke I assumed the conversation was over. Wrong.

"This isn't about the sales meeting, is it?"

"Don't start." I sighed. "Not now."

"This is your passive-aggressive way of punishing me because I told you I don't want to have kids."

I sighed again. "Dr. Phil, can we please save the psycho-babble for another time? Let's just go to your place." I rubbed my hand along Monica's thigh. "Maybe a tired brother could even get a back rub?"

She removed my hand. "I've never lied to you, Tony. I told you from the moment it seemed like we were getting serious. Marriage? Maybe. Kids? No. Period. Not open to negotiation."

I interrupted her before she could finish. I'd heard the story before. "You raised your brothers and sisters and you have no interest in raising anymore kids. It's your turn."

I pulled the car into the underground parking lot of the high-rise condominium building where she lived. "But nobody's turn lasts forever."

"Don't mock me, Tony."

"I'm sorry if you feel that way because I'm not mocking you." I pushed the knob that shut down the engine. "But you'd make a great mom."

"That's not the point."

"Can we just go upstairs?"

She shook her head.

"You want to grab a bag and come to my place then?" That would be even better. I didn't look forward to fighting rush hour traffic in the morning. Once again Monica shook her head. "Okay, what do you want to do? Stay out here in the garage all night?"

"I want us to go to Jamaica and have a good time just like we planned. Okay? Please? You deserve a little R&R." She wrapped her arms around my neck.

I kissed the top of her head. "You're so beautiful," I whispered in her ear. I felt myself getting hard.

"So, are you going to have time to pick up your suit from Macy's or would you like me to?"

The girl was working it. She wasn't the first high-powered sales person I'd been involved with. What was that technique called? A presumptive close? Did she think I'd fall for that? I wondered what she'd try next. A Ben Franklin close? Have me list all the pros of going on one side of a piece of paper and the cons on the other?

I kissed the nape of her neck in just the spot that I knew caused her to get moist. "Babe, don't we have a good thing?" We could both use a little distressing. I could tell she was wound as tight as a spring.

She stepped away from me. "Honey-bunny, we have a very good thing." She took my hand into her own and nestled our clasped grip between her breasts. She wasn't playing fair. "Tony, the trip is only three days. Brenda's not due for another month. Very few first time pregnancies are early. And if she was going to miscarry that would have happened by now." Blink, blink, blink, blink, blink, blink.

I didn't disagree with anything she had said.

She planted a soft, wet kiss on my lips then massaged my temple in a circular motion with the tips of her index fingers. She was the only woman I'd ever known who could make my migraine go away with just her touch. I closed my eyes and felt the pressure receding like the tide from my brain. I had never said it out loud but I knew I could fall in love with this woman. I hugged her to my chest. "If you were eight month's pregnant I would never leave you to go on a business trip." She pushed away from me.

"But we'll never be in that position. Remember, I'm never going to get pregnant."

Monica released my hand and looked into my eyes. God, she looked sexy. I hadn't done it in the back seat of a car since high school but I might not be able to wait until we got upstairs. "So if I told you I'd been poking holes in the rubbers before we had sex, what would you do? Have an abortion if you found out you were pregnant?"

Even as the sound of drums started to pound in the

back of my head again as my headache returned, I chuckled at the look of utter horror that crossed her face. "I'm kidding," I assured her. "I'm kidding. Really, I'm kidding," I repeated a third time before she finally relaxed.

"That wasn't funny."

"I'm sorry." I took her hand and tried to lead her toward the elevator. "Come on." She wouldn't move. She stayed rooted to the spot where she stood.

"Answer me, Tony. Are you going on my incentive trip? Yes or no?"

"I've already told you."

"Tell me again. Yes or no."

"No."

"Then it's over."

"Monica, come on."

She shook her head. "I mean it."

"Okay, let me just come up and get my things."

She shook her head again. "I'll messenger them to your place in the morning."

"So it's like that?"

"Yes, it's like that."

"You're sure about this?"

"I don't deserve to be punished for wanting what I want."

"Sorry you feel that way." I handed her the keys to the Demon. I opened my mouth to speak but she shook her head. "Don't say anything." She twirled around and ran toward the elevator.

I watched as the steel doors of the garage elevator slammed shut. I took a deep breath then searched the garage for my car. No wonder men had such strong attachments with their automobiles. In a lifetime of car ownership my ride had never broken my heart.

# Chapter 5 – Maya

I walked into my condo and kicked off my shoes. It was good to be home. Five a.m. would roll around quickly and that's the time I got up every day to go to work. I liked being first in the office. If the old saying that the early bird catches the worm is true I wanted to be first in line at the worm buffet.

As I sat in the middle of my rice planter bed positioned to take full advantage of my thirtieth story view, I hoped I'd be able to fall asleep. I loved the feel of the eight hundred thread count Egyptian cotton sheets against my skin. I had seen the exact same set at Bloomingdales for seven hundred dollars but I got these on eBay for a hundred. I closed my eyes and tried to clear my mind of the thoughts that kept popping up like kernels of popcorn.

"Ohm." I chanted the meditation mantra I had learned during the *Science of the Breath* class I'd taken the summer after my mother died. "Ohm, ohm, ohm."

I sat with my hands folded in my lap as she had taught me to do when I was a little girl and forced to sit through both Sunday morning services, the eight and the eleven o'clock, at New Salem Missionary Baptist Church on the corner of Cleveland Avenue and Morning Glory Lane. The sanctuary vibrated with the mighty voices of the choir that was too large to stay contained within the confines of its stone walls. From the lushness of the sound that tumbled over the pulpit and rolled beyond the pews until it spilled on the asphalt in front of the church, one voice always soared above the others. The sweet soprano of my mother was strong and clear.

I tried to pull my thoughts away from my childhood memories without success. I continued to see the church that erupted like a volcano all around me. Ladies in white uniforms and nurse's shoes racing from one fallen body to the next, dispensing fans emblazoned with images of local funeral homes, swabbing sweaty brows with freshly starched handkerchiefs complements of the Senior Ladies Guild while my mother sang in a voice that mesmerized and surprised me on Sunday mornings. It seemed so odd that her Sunday morning voice had such power. But like her choir robe, after service, she packed it away and didn't bring it back out until the next time she was called upon to sing.

At least once a month even the pastor, Reverend Grayson, would be swept away in the euphoria of the moment. Like a gazelle, he'd circle around the church, his robe floating around him like a black rain cloud. I always wanted to turn around in my seat. I wanted to watch his progress around the church but I felt the stern admonishment of my mother. "Sit still. Be a good girl. Don't embarrass me."

When he returned to the pulpit, sweat poured from his brow. "Sister Latimer, I ain't going to let you sing no mo' cause when you do, look what happens." The pastor spread wide his arms indicating the pandemonium in the Lord's house. "I ain't going to even try to preach. I might as well go ahead and open the doors to the church."

I watched my mother beam from the choir stand. I listened as people shouted her name and begged her to keep singing. Even the pastor's voice would take on a sing-song quality as he spoke, "Is there anybody out there who don't know what it is that Sister Latimer is singing about?"

I didn't know but I knew better than to raise my hand. Though I didn't know what she was singing about, that wasn't the question to which I longed for an answer. What I wondered was why, after all the shouting and jubilation, after all the love that rained down upon my mother on the Sunday mornings when she sang, why after church service did we always go home alone?

# Chapter 6 – Maya

The first streaks of sunlight painted the sky as I pulled into the underground parking garage of Narcisco Industries. Our corporate offices occupied prime Chicago loop real estate and screamed to the world that we were *the shit*. And since I worked for them I must be the shit as well.

Narcisco occupied the seventieth through eighty-fifth floor of the polished steel and glass tower that housed the select few individuals tasked with developing the strategic vision that lower-level minions of the corporation were sent forth to implement.

My heels clicked like castanets as I strolled across the cavernous polished marble entry way to the guard desk. Three African-American females guarded the entrance as if they were the offspring of Zeus and his wife, Themis, who like in Greek mythology had the power to control the destiny of mere mortals.

"May I help you?" asked the youngest of the three guards. Her gold tooth sparkled in the morning sun that spilled into the atrium. Her accent was so thick that if she were a character in a movie, each time she spoke on screen her lines would have included subtitles.

I pushed aside my ambivalence and flashed her my company identification card and brightest smile, the smile meant to express solidarity to the sisterhood even though I had about as much in common with this woman as I did with Jane Goodall, the white woman who lived in Africa studying apes.

But unlike Lillian who had definitively concluded "neck-snapping-mush-mouth-talking-with-three-or-four-different-baby-daddy" black women like the stereotype represented by the trio of security guards cast negative aspersions on *all* black women, and therefore should be avoided, I was less sure of how to interact with them. The black women I'd encountered throughout my career were never in peer-level positions. In all my years of working, Donna was the only black female co-worker I'd ever had who was at the same pay grade. And even she and I worked in different disciplines, and now worked in different facilities, and were different levels. Once again, I was the only one.

"I work for Narcisco Industries," I said to the guard.

She looked at me as if to say, so fucking what?

If I were Donna, in less than a couple of weeks me and this threesome would be bosom buddies or, at least, bosom acquaintances. For most corporate executives, women like the guards or the cleaning people or the folks who came and watered the plants were invisible, but for Donna they were allies and informants and sometimes even casual friends.

Though my feelings leaned more toward Donna's

than Lillian's, I didn't share the same degree of bone-deep comfort she had in associating with whomever she desired in the work place. "Why, just because I'm black," she asked, "do I have to carry the weight of every ignorant black person on this planet on my back? You think when white women see some poor-white-trash-no-front-teeth-had-a-baby-by-her-daddy-hillbilly-white-sandal-shoe-wearing-in-the-winter-time-heiffer, they feel any sense of shame? You think they think that bitch is making white women look bad? Hell no! Well me either."

So though I didn't feel a need to ostracize myself, I did feel a little ashamed.

"Starting today I'll be working here on the eightieth floor. For Narcisco." Until this assignment I had worked in our suburban regional Midwest facility. Before that I'd done a stint in Atlanta after my first assignment in San Antonio. I pushed my badge closer to the guard who in turn pushed the visitor's log toward me.

"You need to sign in."

"But I'm not a visitor. I'm already a Narcisco Industries employee. It's just that starting today I'll be working from this location instead of Schaumburg."

The guard imitated the slightly exaggerated slowness in the way I had spoken to her when she responded. "Until you get a badge from this location, you still a visitor. So sign in or step out of the way."

A little crowd had gathered behind me as people waited to be scanned into the building. One of the other guards tapped Miss Gold Tooth on the shoulder.

"LaQuicia, there he is," she whispered.

Our conversation ended immediately as the guard tilted her head toward the bank of revolving doors in front of the building. LaQuicia and I turned in the direction her comrade indicated. People flowed like a stream around me, their badges beeping admittance to

*Surrender to Love*

the start of their work day. I was surprised that so many other people started work this early. Now that I was playing in the major leagues, I'd have to step up my game.

An African-American man in a brown UPS uniform that showed off his well muscled arms and ironing board flat stomach strolled across the lobby.

"Hey, Tony," called out LaQuicia.

Tony turned toward the guard station.

"Get yo' new badge today. Now, go on." LaQuicia had lost all interest in me. She waved me toward the elevators in dismissal.

The man tipped an imaginary hat in salute to the women at the guard desk.

"Hey Tony," the guards called out in unison. LaQuicia walked to the far edge of the guard desk and blew Tony a kiss.

"You looking awfully good today, LaQuicia. You must have a hot date tonight."

"You so silly," she laughed.

"Hey," he called out. "Hold that elevator."

I pushed the hold button as he sprinted across the lobby. He stepped inside the elevator with a two-wheeler laden with packages.

"You're new here," he said to me. It was a statement, not a question.

"First day." I pressed the button for the eightieth floor.

"Let me guess." He did an imitation of Auguste Rodin's statue *The Thinker* then said, "Human Resources for Narcisco?"

"How'd you know?" From my reaction, you would've thought he'd executed a David Blane-style magic trick.

"I've been working this building for a while. Eightieth floor is human resources and legal for Narcisco; seventy-ninth through seventy-five is marketing; seventy through seventy-four is research and development and who the hell knows what you guys do on the eighty-first floor and above. We lowly delivery men aren't allowed up there."

"So how'd you know I wasn't in legal?"

He smiled. "I've met quite a few folks from legal. Some of them are really cool and all, but all are super-super conservative." He placed extra emphasis on the word *super*. "Believe me nobody in legal is rocking Roberto Cavalli."

My gaze narrowed as I stared more intently at this guy. Was I being punked? Was he the black guy from Ashton Kutcher's television show? I took a closer look. The brother on the show was okay but this UPS man was fine with a capital *F*.

I scanned the front of my outfit hoping I hadn't inadvertently gone Minnie Pearl and left a label on the front of my jacket. Nope. In fact, the designer-resale shop where I'd found this outfit normally cut the labels out. "You're just a regular Houdini, huh?"

I averted my gaze from the muscle that bulged in his arm as he shifted the cart to his left hand and extended his right one to shake mine.

"What's your name, by the way? I'm Tony. Tony Jackson."

I accepted his hand. His grip was firm. "Maya. Maya Latimer." I felt my stomach rise to the top of my chest as the elevator doors sprung open. At least I wanted to believe it was the abruptness of the elevator's stopping and not the way he was smiling at me that made me feel this way.

"Who're you looking for? I can escort you." He wheeled the dolly off the elevator with one hand.

"Aren't you just too kind?"

"Company policy. We try harder."

"I thought that was Avis."

I looked around the floor to see which of the corner offices seemed unoccupied. I felt like strutting down the aisle George Jefferson from the nineteen-seventies television show, *The Jefferson's*, style.

"You got me, Ms. Maya Latimer, that is Avis." Once again he tipped his imaginary hat in deference. "Don't forget I am at your service. Let me know if you need anything."

"I'll do that, Mr. Jackson."

As I walked down the hall I noticed that I wasn't the only woman who appreciated our UPS man's physique.

# Chapter 7 – Maya

I felt like a cat mesmerized by a shiny bauble. I had to consciously force myself to look away from the diamond cufflinks on my new boss, James Caplin's, custom tailored French cuff shirt. If I continued staring at them I might be blinded by the bling. Though only in his early forties, I knew he made big bucks. Like my salary was less than his annual bonus. And evidently, he enjoyed spending the money he earned; Patek Philippe wristwatch; Gucci gray striped suit with Jacquard stitching; teamed with a pair of black slip-on Varvatos to prove he didn't have to try too hard. Everything didn't have to be couture.

I might not have as many contacts as Donna, but I didn't need them since Donna was one of my sources. A few hours after I'd asked her to find out whatever she could about my new boss, we had sat in the company cafeteria for a debrief.

"He grew up on Long Island. Old money."

I nodded. That meant that his family had vacationed in the Hampton's long before money was the only requirement necessary to associate with the beautiful people there.

"Word on the street is that he doesn't care if a few rules get bent to deliver the results."

That didn't surprise me. He was a legend for producing a six year record of double-digit earnings and annual bonuses that paid out at well over one hundred percent to target. I had seen the checks. My department processed them. So maybe my Republican was showing because I felt one had the right to a few fuck-ups when they were putting that kind of money in people's pockets.

"This stint heading up human resources is supposed to teach him a few lessons before he lands the company in deep shit. I couldn't get all the details but there are a few sexual harassment skeletons in his closet, so watch yourself."

I thanked my girl for her insight. None of it surprised me. I knew that leading the human resources effort for someone like James Caplin could be a mine field but I wanted a chance to skate close to the edge. The wealthiest people in America, maybe the world, had roots that were not completely clean. Stay close to the fire without being burned. But in the new millennium, even those rules had evolved. Martha Stewart, among others, showed that one could survive, even thrive, after a little roasting. Play with fire as long as you're not consumed by the flames. My boss had mastered that skill and I wanted to learn it from him. No more Miss Nice Gal for me.

He propped his feet on top of the desk he had imported from East Indonesia. It was made of macassar ebony. The varied hues of dark brown against the black background were stunning. He peered at me down the long, straight nose that people assumed had come from years of breeding the best of the best East Coast blue blood but had actually been helped by the assistance of a surgeon's scalpel. How Donna had found that out I'd never know. I didn't even ask.

"Mr. Caplin?"

"James."

"James," I corrected myself. "I just want to thank you for your vote of confidence."

He held up a manicured hand like a stop signal and cut me off. "Believe me, no need to thank me. I'll make you earn this promotion."

"No problem." I smiled. "There's no challenge I can't handle."

"Watch his ass," Donna had warned me. "People say he's like a shark. If he smells weakness he'll attack just for the sheer joy of watching you flail around." She told me more than one rising young star's career had been sidetracked to the junkyard after riding the rails with James Caplin as conductor. I had no intention of suffering such a fate. I had prepared my entire life for this opportunity and I was going to grab it and ride it to my own pot of gold.

"Let me be blunt."

"Please."

"Have you heard that Narcisco might be acquired?"

Before I responded I did a quick mental assessment of the political correctness of my answer. Of course I had heard the rumors. But if I admitted to it, would that make me seem like a gossip? But if I said that I wasn't aware of the scuttle-butt, would that make me seem out of the loop? I knew formal and informal communication was of equal importance to one's success in corporate America. Like a slave seeking freedom on the underground railroad, if you missed the subtle, often unspoken, cues that the train was coming, you could miss a chance that might never come around again.

"Yes, I've heard that. Is it true?" If James liked people to be blunt. I could do blunt.

His smile was almost imperceptible when he nodded.

I was confident my countenance revealed nothing of what I felt inside — sheer jubilation. I had read several analyst reports that said if the speculated acquisition of Narcisco Industries by Musikiwa International was consummated, the merger would produce one of the fastest run-ups in stock value in the history of the market. Over the years I had bought as much stock as company policy allowed. At today's stock price I had a tidy little sum set aside, even after paying the medical bills my mother's insurance policy didn't cover.

"I'm planning to retire at fifty," he continued. "This acquisition holds the key."

The notion of not working seemed as foreign to me as Tagalog even though the Filipino language was spoken by over sixty-five million people.

"And I always get what I want." His gaze was so intense I was forced to look away before he recognized my confusion. Were we still talking about Musikiwa?

"We have over one thousand management employees. I need profiles on each of them. The executives from Musikiwa need to assess staffing levels when the acquisition goes through. Their organization is extremely lean."

"Did you say when? Not if?" Trade papers hypothesized that Musikiwa was the leading candidate in the race to deliver a vaccine to protect women against breast cancer. The engineers at Narcisco were developing the device that could be the best means for drug delivery.

"It depends." James planted his feet on the floor with a thud. "On whether we can deliver what they want when they want it." He leaned forward, his steel blue eyes seemed to bore a hole through my jacket. "Can we?"

"I'll do my part." I stood. "When do you need them?"

"A week."

"A week?"

"A week."

"Then a week is more than enough time for my staff and me."

# Chapter 8 – Maya

I turned on the light switch in my new office and gasped. First, because the view outside my window was breathtaking. The sun reflected against the waves of Lake Michigan that danced below me like the thousand points of light promised but never delivered by a former president. So though the view was enough to cause a colored girl from the southside to lose her breath, the second reason I did a double take was because my desk and almost every inch of the floor was covered with crates packed with binders. My assistant, Maggie, stuck her head in the office. Her red hair floated like a cloud around her head that seemed overly large, probably because of the upswept hairdo she sported. "The rest of the files are at the copy center.

They should be sent over by noon."

"You mean there's more?"

"Yes ma'am."

"Set up a meeting with my staff in an hour. It's mandatory that everyone's there. We've got a lot of work to get done."

She nodded.

I looked at the clock on the only surface of my office that was not either a window or glass. "Eleven o'clock." I took off my jacket, rolled up my sleeves and looked at the labels on each of the binders. I organized them into piles then ripped the cellophane off a new package of audio tapes and popped one into a small hand held recorder.

"Binder one," I said into the tape, "Engineering."

Maggie knocked on my closed office door. "Do you need anything else before I call it a day?"

I looked up at the clock. It was six thirty-five. Already? I hadn't taken a break since my meeting. "Do we have more tapes?"

She nodded.

Speaking into a tape recorder was a trick I'd learned from the mentor who had been assigned to work with me when I entered the ninth grade. I was impressed by the woman who had chosen me, a tall African-American who personified the expression blue-black when referencing skin tone. She seemed the epitome of who I wanted to become when I grew up — articulate, well-groomed, financially successful, respected. Though I admired my mentor, Zoë Mitchell, I discontinued participation in the program after only two sessions.

Though my guidance counselor begged me not to quit, after I read the program description, *high potential students from disadvantaged homes are teamed with high-powered executives, working with them in the development of life strategies that can lead to future success*, I concluded that the disadvantage of being labeled "disadvantaged" outweighed the potential advantage of anything I might gain.

But I took away one little gem from my second and final meeting at Zoë's plush downtown office, that was coincidentally only a few blocks from the office where my name was now engraved on the metallic name plate outside the door, the advice — Never leave anything to chance; never get caught in a situation when it's your word against somebody else's because no matter how successful you become, never forget, when you are black and female some people will always be more equal than you. I had nodded in feigned understanding but it was not until years later that I fully comprehended the wisdom of the counsel I had been given.

Not until I heard my white male co-workers repeat, sometimes verbatim, a statement I had made earlier that barely created a ripple when I said it receive high praise when the words fell from their lips. It was not until I managed the largest plant closure in our region's history, in record time and without litigation though there were union issues and threats of age and gender discrimination, but my white male boss, rather than celebrate my achievement as he did with all my white male co-workers, wondered out loud whether it was hard work or luck that led to my success.

It wasn't until I discovered I made almost twenty thousand dollars less than another white male co-worker who didn't have an advanced degree, though a Masters was supposedly a requisite for all senior manager positions, and his region was about half the size of my own that I truly understood Zoë's advice.

But once I did, I made sure I was never caught in a compromising position. I mastered the art of appearing open and accessible while sharing nothing of myself. I followed the most conservative interpretation of the rules while seeming to be bold and daring, and most of all, the line coined by New York designer

Donna Karan for *Dry Idea* deodorant was created for me. I never let them see me sweat.

"I'll get you another package." Maggie disappeared then reappeared with three packages of tapes in her hands. "This ought to hold you for awhile."

Three hours later I was interrupted by another knock.

"Hungry?"

I clicked off the tape recorder and looked at the clock."As a matter of fact, I am."

James Caplin held two large brown paper bags. "This is the best Thai food in town."

I cleared a space on the top of my desk. He spread out the plastic plates and forks. I would have never guessed him the type of manager who would be thoughtful enough to bring dinner for one of his underlings.

"You've made a lot of progress." He scooped a generous helping of vegetarian pad Thai onto the plate in front of me. "I hope you like things spicy."

And I, especially, would not have believed him to be the type of man willing to serve someone, especially someone who was not only black but female and a subordinate. "Still have a good ways to go," I said.

"If there's anything that I can help you with just let me know. I don't believe in asking anything of my staff that I'm not willing to do myself."

"Thanks. I appreciate that." Maybe the rumors about him being an asshole weren't true. In my twelve year career with Narcisco I'd had my share of asshole managers and co-workers but none had ever volunteered to help me with a project.

"Work hard, play hard." He stood and pulled a bottle of expensive Chardonnay from one of the paper bags. Next he removed two long stemmed wine glasses. "I never drink out of plastic."

I shook my head as he filled a glass for me. "No, I can't."

He ignored my protests and held the glass of golden liquid toward me."Afraid someone might tell the boss?"

We both smiled."Well, okay." I shrugged. "I was about to pack up and call it a night anyway."

He lifted his glass. "Cheers."

I touched the side of my glass to his. "Cheers," I repeated.

# Chapter 9 – Maya

"Good morning."

"Morning," I said. I accepted the cup of coffee my assistant, Maggie, handed me. She had made a point of stocking my favorite brand and kept a pot perked and on the ready. I tried to stifle a yawn but I was tired. It seemed like I had just left this place. Maybe because I had only been absent for a few hours. But I wasn't being paid to lounge around the house eating in bonbons. I had a job to do and I was well compensated to make it happen.

Now that I made more money than I had ever imagined, more things became free. Now that I could afford to pay the exorbitant underground garage parking fees, I was given a monthly allowance to cover the expense. Now when I could afford to spend money on lunches at the fancy downtown restaurants we frequented, all charges went on my corporate credit card and were automatically paid. I would never even see a bill.

"Did you sleep here?" asked Maggie. "I thought I was an early bird."

"I should have," I said. I'd been here since three o'clock in the morning. At least, today, I had been the earliest bird. There was no one else at the guard desk waiting to be granted entry.

"Maya Latimer?"

Maggie and I both looked up. I fell into a pair of dark brown eyes and smiled. Maggie frowned. The owner of the rich baritone was Tony, the UPS man.

"I have a package for you."

"You can leave it on my desk," began Maggie.

"That's okay, Maggie, I can handle this."

She nodded but I could tell she wasn't pleased. If Tony weren't Tony I wouldn't be either. But since he was Tony, I added,"close my door on your way out."

Only with great effort was I able to pull my gaze from the muscles in his arm. I needed to get laid. It had been too long. I looked away from Tony and hoped he hadn't noticed the blush that started at the nape of my neck and worked its way to my forehead.

"So you all settled in?"

"Getting there."

I wondered if the air conditioner had stopped working. The temperature in my office had heated up at least five degrees.

"You know if you ever need an extra pair of hands, I'm here to offer my services." He held up his hands. The nails were trimmed but not professionally manicured. I wondered how they'd feel caressing my body. I felt a heaviness in my lower regions that needed to be addressed.

"Aren't you just too kind?"

I saw Maggie watching us. Glass offices maintained

a high tech look but the lack of privacy was a definite down side.

"A good man does what he can."

"I wouldn't know. I've met so few."

Tony stumbled backwards as though he'd been stabbed. "Ouch." He made a motion as if pulling a knife from his chest.

I laughed. I liked his sense of humor. "Sorry, nothing personal."

"Yeah, yeah, we good brothers have it rough."

"Seriously, please accept my apology."

"Isn't your boyfriend a good man?"

I couldn't give him points for being smooth. That's for sure. That line reminded me of a high school move, like when a boy faked a yawn to get his arm around a girl's shoulder at the movies. But I had to give Mr. Jackson points for looking so damned cute when he asked the question. I was flattered that he even wondered. "My boyfriend and I broke up a few months ago."

"No wonder you're down on men. He was a fool."

I smiled. I heard Lillian's voice asking what the hell was I doing. I'm a senior executive. This man is the hired help. Of course, UPS was a pretty big company. Both our employers were members of the Fortune 500 club. But I knew that counted for nothing with Lillian. "Just because you're both black doesn't give every brother on the planet liberties. You think these Negroes filling the vending machines or tearing up the sidewalks are stepping to Miss Anne like that? It's an insult, girlfriend. You need to recognize."

I understood Lillian's point but Tony was the first guy in a long time who had made me feel tingly inside.

"I like to think of him that way," I said in response to his comment about Deuce. Deuce was a fool. And an asshole.

"I better let you get back to work," he said. I could tell he didn't want to leave any more than I was ready

*Surrender to Love*

for him to go but I did have work to do and he was on a schedule.

"Before my assistant breaks her neck trying to hear what we're talking about in here."

Tony's hand rested on the door knob but he didn't turn it. "Hey, you into house music?"

"You mean hip-hop?"

He shook his head. "No, I mean house."

"Not really."

He chuckled. "I've seen that blank stare before. You've never experienced house music."

"Is that so?" My social life was in a sorry state. This conversation was the best time I'd had with a man since before I broke up with Deuce.

"That's what I think."

Maggie knocked on the door.

"Excuse me. Sorry to interrupt. Mr. Caplin just called. He needs to see you. It's urgent."

She closed the door.

"Duty calls."

"Go on girl, handle your business."

I wondered if Maggie saw me watching his ass as he walked out of my office.

# Chapter 10 – Maya

Though it was close to midnight, on a week night, the north side neighborhood still buzzed with activity as I pulled into the parking lot of the downtown Trader Joe's grocery store. I was a coffeeholic and couldn't wait until I got to the office for my first cup and I was completely out of the Viennese roasted Arabica beans I coveted.

I scanned the shelves of exotic coffee beans and tried to ignore the mini drama playing out at the end of the aisle. There but for the grace of God go I, I thought as I glanced down the aisle at a young blonde woman and her blonde-haired boy.

"Trevor, stop it." The woman pulled a package of ice cream bars from the grasp of a little boy who looked to be about three years old. The baby strapped to the front of her chest gurgled and bobbed up and down.

"M.Y.O.B." I repeated the phrase my mother had coined — mind your own business — but my attention wandered back to the woman and little boy.

"Let go, sweetie." She couldn't have been more than twenty-two or twenty-three. I had to give girlfriend her props. I was impressed at her restraint. She hadn't raised her voice even an octave. She maintained that bedtime story modulation as she wrestled with the boy for custody of the ice cream bars. The cynic in me wondered if she were on Valium. Many women, myself included, would have snatched that ice cream, given him a hard swat on the bottom and told him to shut up and calm his ass down. That's what I say but who knows what I would have done?

"No," shouted the boy.

"Would you mind?"

I looked up and down the aisle."Are you talking to me?"

She nodded. "Could you hold him for a second?" The young mother indicated the baby on her chest. "I really need to deal with this one." She pointed to the head of the three-year-old. "He wouldn't settle down so I thought coming here might tire him out a bit."

I looked at the little boy who stared defiantly at me. I stared back at him. "Guess it didn't work," I said.

The woman made a half hearted attempt at smiling.

I shook my head. "Sorry." I pushed my grocery cart around the threesome. "I'm not good with babies."

In truth I didn't know whether I was or wasn't good with them. Growing up as the only child of an only child I was never around other kids. My mother never let me baby-sit. I wasn't allowed to go over to my friend's houses so I never got to play with their baby brothers or sisters. Given my limited exposure to babies I was surprised by how calm I felt when I first suspected I was pregnant. Though my ex-boyfriend, Deuce, and I had taken precautions, and regardless of what he thought, I wasn't trying to get pregnant. I didn't arbor any unspoken desire to have a baby. He was the one who'd said he wanted more children.

So perhaps because I never thought about having kids, the first week of my missed period I didn't even realize it was late. By the second week I experienced a nagging feeling that I had forgotten to do something. When I remembered that I hadn't marked an *x* on the calendar to signal the start of my period for the month, a habit I had practiced since my period started the summer before I entered six grade, I counted the days since I had marked my last *x*. Thirty-five. Thirty-five days since the start of my last period. I counted the days three more times and each time I counted thirty-five. Thirty five days meant that I was seven days past due. Seven days. I counted the number of days that had elapsed between each of my periods over the past three years, and like clockwork, my period always came on the twenty-eighth day.

When the pregnancy test strip onto which I peed detected human chorionic gonadotropim, the indicator of pregnancy, I was still calm. I didn't panic. I didn't place an emergency call to my girls to set up a tribunal to help me decide what I should do. It felt surreal. According to the evidence I was pregnant. A period that was never late was seven days past due. A procedure that claimed to be almost one hundred accurate tested positive. I was pregnant.

I didn't even call Deuce. He was traveling and we already had plans to get together later that week. The news could wait until then. But it wasn't because I was scared to tell him. I don't know why I didn't call. I just didn't. Even though by the time he came over, I had taken an early pregnancy test two more times and each time confirmed the results of the first. When I finally saw him, the pregnancy wasn't the first thing I mentioned. Even when we made love and he slipped on a condom I didn't tell him there was no longer a need for caution.

As I pushed my grocery cart through Trader Joe's, all of a sudden I felt exhausted. Lack of sleep, or more likely thoughts about Deuce, had caught up with me. I threw a couple packages of coffee beans into my grocery cart and pushed toward the checkout. I had to get home.

"Maya," a voice called. "Maya Latimer!"

Was someone calling me? I couldn't stop the smile that spread across my face when I recognized the owner of that voice. I felt renewed energy.

"Hey there."

"Hey there yourself. Tony, right?" I don't know why I did that. I remembered his name. He was no longer in his UPS uniform and sported a pair of ripped blue jeans that hugged his thighs like a lover. A white French cuffed shirt was open to reveal the perfect amount of hair on his chest. He was even better looking than I remembered. To say that he was tall, dark and handsome was an understatement.

"Wait a second." He pushed his grocery cart closer to me. "This must be my lucky night."

"You never know." The thought of going into my empty apartment felt unbearable. Besides, I deserved a little reward. And if the bulge in the front of his pants were a true indicator the reward might not be too small. An orgasm was the best kind of sleeping aid. My smile froze, however, when I realized the woman who appeared to be ready to give birth any second was with him. I looked at the woman's swollen belly then back to Tony. "I've got to go." My tone was as chilly as the freezer cases from which I had just walked away.

"Wait a minute."

"Didn't you hear the woman?" I knew she was speaking loud enough for me to hear her. "She said she had to go. Let her go."

Well, girlfriend didn't have to worry about me. I'd had my fill of complicated relationships. She could have him.

# Chapter 11 – Maya

Though I might regret it later, I poured myself a large glass of wine. What the hell was wrong with me? Why should I care who the UPS-man was at the grocery store with? Just as I sat down the phone rang. I looked at the clock. I knew who it was even before I checked the caller I.D.

"Hey girl," I said. "I was just thinking about calling you."

"So you weren't asleep?" Lillian asked.

Though it was almost one o'clock in the morning and I needed to be asleep, I knew this would be another restless night. "Thanks again for the other night," I said. I hoped she couldn't tell I felt out of sorts. I wasn't in the mood for anymore armchair analysis even if I had come to agree with her. I needed to start acting like the corporate executive I was.

"It was like old times, wasn't it?"

I nodded and sipped my wine. "Since you up and quit to enter the world of full-time wifedom and motherhood we just don't get to see each other enough." And since the"procedure" as the staff at the clinic called it, I had only seen her twice prior to our get-together. I still felt too conflicted about it all. If Lillian, the woman I would have voted most unlikely to enter motherhood, could be a good, no, a *great* mother, could I have been? Even if it meant raising a child alone? My mother had done it. Her mother had done it. Lord knows the majority of black women in America were doing it, and with fewer resources than me.

"I'd love to get together more often but you know Rick's schedule." Lillian sighed.

"And so did you when you married him." I didn't normally play the I-told-you-so game but lately I had a lot less patience with her. Was it guilt? Or jealousy that her man loved her enough to marry her? To take care of her? To make babies with her? Wasn't I good enough for a man to want that with me?

"You're right." Her façade of gloom evaporated. "So, let me live vicariously through you. How's the job? You like your new boss? Met anybody? I loved working downtown. I do kind of miss the hustle and bustle of the city."

I drained my glass before I answered. "Job's fine, busy as hell but I expected that. Jury is still out on the boss. Heard a lot of ugly things about him before I started but so far, he's cool. A little intense, but okay." I debated whether I should share the last tidbit of information with her.

"Go on. I can tell you're holding out."

"I have met somebody. Kind of ..."

"Ooh details," squealed Lillian.

"The UPS driver."

"The UPS driver?"

"Yes, the UPS driver."

"Stop it. I don't want to even hear it."

"He's as fine as hell."

"Girl, you are not in high school. What he looks like doesn't matter."

"How much he makes should be my only concern?"

"You know that's not what I meant. But hell yes, how much he makes does matter."

Though everyone laughed when Lillian unwrapped my baby shower gift, a DVD of the movie *Waiting to Exhale*, my warning that she not end up like the Bernadine character was not a joke. You can't depend on these niggers.

"Men lie. And men hurt you. You got to know that."

My mother told me that on the first day of my first period and repeated it over the years more times than I could count. I had nodded and promised her I would not forget that. Though, of course, time and time again, I did.

"Are you listening to me?" demanded Lillian.

My girl was getting on my nerves. I was ready to hang up. It was late and I was tired. "Girlfriend, how many times do I have to tell you that I'm not looking for a husband? I don't want a meaningful relationship. Or someone to pay my mortgage. I just want somebody to kick it with every now and then." I poured more wine into my glass.

"Don't convict every man of being like Deuce before you even give yourself a chance to find out what he's really about."

"All right, Oprah."

Though Lillian and Donna knew my breakup with Deuce was painful, they had no idea how devastated I was when he told me, in fact when he and his *wife*, Sandy, told me, holding hands, looking like a set of salt and pepper shakers, that Deuce was not leaving her, his wife, but that he was, in fact, leaving me, his mistress.

Three days after I told him I was pregnant, and he

accused me of being a manipulative bitch, he asked if he could come by. I said yes and thought thank God the clinic hadn't been able to schedule my *procedure* for two weeks from the time I'd called. I should've known after he cooled down he'd do the right thing. He loved me. He'd told me so. Over and over again.

So when I opened the door, for several seconds I wondered who the plain, chubby, sandy-haired white woman standing next to him was. I had only seen her one time and that had been from a distance, once when we were having lunch at an out-of-the-way downtown bistro and decided to be seated at the wrought iron tables the restaurant had set up on the street. At first, I thought he had found something distasteful in his food when I saw his changed expression.

"You okay?"

"Here comes my wife."

"What? Where?"

"Blue dress, thick blonde hair."

I glanced at the woman with whom Deuce had shared ten years of married life. After six years in the military, he'd used his GI bill to attend college full time.

That's where he met Sandy, serious, studious, compassionate Sandy. They married the year after she graduated. He claimed the instant they left the sanctuary of their Ivy League campus, he knew it was a mistake, but he couldn't leave her. She had sacrificed too much for their relationship for him to desert her. She had lost her slice of her grandfather's inheritance, though it had been reinstated when they produced the second sandy-haired child, both of whom, if Deuce was not around, could have passed for white. I had seen her that day but she hadn't seen us. I wondered what she thought of me. Was I what she pictured his mistress would like?

"May we come in?" Deuce held Sandy's hand as they walked into my condo, the place that had been the primary backdrop for our lovemaking.

"Let me get right to the point," he said.

I sat while they continued to stand. I didn't offer them a seat.

"I told Sandy everything."

When I looked at her, I wanted to slap that smug smile off her face as she stood there, holding his hand, caressing the top of it with her thumb.

"We discussed it and decided if you don't want to have an abortion ..."

"I'm a woman," Sandy interjected, "A feminist. I understand that choice means having a complete spectrum of options in the decisions a woman makes concerning her body."

Who did she think she was talking to? I wasn't one of the women to whom she provided free life coaching.

"Sandy and I will adopt the baby." I looked from Deuce to Sandy who smiled encouragingly at him. Had they lost their minds?

"Traditional adoption, not open." She seemed almost embarrassed that her generosity had boundaries.

I poured myself another glass of wine and tuned back to Lillian's conversation. "Seriously, you're not twenty-five anymore."

"You're right, girlfriend" I said. "So, my old ass needs some sleep. Talk to you later." I hung up the phone before she could protest.

# Chapter 12 – Tony

"Thanks," I said to the tall brunette who held the elevator door long enough for me to glide in. I knew Maya had seen me but refused to make eye contact. When the last passenger got off and just the two of us remained, I said, "You ran off so quickly yesterday I didn't have a chance to introduce you to my sister."

"Your sister?"

"Yeah, my sister. She's going through a pretty rough time. Her husband was killed in Iraq three weeks ago."

Maya's hand flew to her heart. "Oh my God, I'm so sorry."

"So big brother is stepping in."

"You really are trying to make a believer out of me, aren't you?"

"Huh?"

*Surrender to Love*

"That you're one of the good guys."

I laughed. The elevator door opened. On impulse I said, "I want to take you somewhere tonight."

She shook her head but I wasn't taking no for an answer. "My favorite MC is playing at this little house music club on the north side. Come with me."

"Thanks, but I can't."

"Why? You on punishment?"

I had spent enough time around women to know, no matter how much money they made, how many degrees they had earned or even how attractive they were, a brother who wasn't intimidated to step to them had a chance. Black, white, Hispanic, Asian, it didn't matter. Pimpology 101, the art of understanding the female psyche.

"Pick you up at nine o'clock?" I could tell she was considering it."Where do you live?" I held out a clip board with a blank packing slip. She hesitated for a second then wrote down her address. I winked at her and nodded."Wear something funky."

## Chapter 13 – Maya

As if in a hypnotic state people moved frenetically across the dance floor to the steady rhythm of the house music beat that blared through the sound system of a club that started its life as a garage. Steel beams, a polished concrete floor, a glass bar that seemed to float on invisible wires made the space utilitarian but unique.

"This place is fabulous," I screamed to be heard over the noise.

Tony smiled. His head bobbed in rhythm with the music.

"Hey, Tony," said a waitress wearing black leather biker shorts, ripped fish net stockings and bustier.

"Hey, Heather."

Tony and the waitress hugged. He pulled my stool closer to him. "Heather, this is my lady Maya."

When I looked at her I wondered which had hurt more; the body piercings or the tattoos. She winked at me and gave me the thumbs up signal. "He's a good one," she shouted.

"Thanks." After the words escaped my lips I wondered for what I was thanking her.

"Bring me a Kettle One martini and my lady will have..." Tony looked at me so that I could finish the sentence.

"A chardonnay. Very dry."

"You got it."

The waitress disappeared into the crowded dance floor.

"You must be a regular here." I was surprised that I felt a twinge of jealousy at Tony's warm embrace of the waitress, as well as a sense of pride that I was sitting next to him. He was the most attractive man in the club. There wasn't even a close second.

"So is this where you bring all your dates?" I hoped I sounded nonchalant. He pulled my stool even closer to him. I felt the warmth of his breath in my ear. "I've never brought another babe here. Just me or me and one of my fellas."

I wouldn't admit how happy that revelation made me. "To what do I owe this honor?"

Before he responded, the waitress returned with our drinks. He slipped a twenty dollar bill on the tray and waved her away as she fished in her coin purse for change. He clicked the side of my wine glass and took a sip.

"So how long have you worked for UPS?" I felt a little too comfortable with the silence between us.

"I started the summer of my freshman year at Georgia State."

"In Atlanta?"

He nodded.

I made a mental note to inform Lillian my UPS-man

had attended college. Not that it was any of her business.

"You know, working at UPS was just a temporary thing."

I nodded again.

"Then my boss at the time, cool dude named Roscoe, one of the first black managers at the facility where I was working told me he could get me on full time. Said he was proud of me and my potential." Tony sipped his drink. "I decided I'd stay, save a little more money for college, start school in January. Then one thing led to another and now, fifteen years later, here I am."

"It's never too late."

"For what?" He looked at me over the top of his glass.

I wasn't sure. What had I meant? Too late for him to make something of his life? Too late for him to move beyond a job that was just a step above a menial laborer? Too late to ascend to my expectations of what my man should be doing for a living? I had dated enough men to know Tony was head and shoulders above most them, even if their credentials on paper were more impressive.

There was the attorney with both a JD and MBA from Loyola University whose father was a surgeon and his mother a high school principal who was still so angry with his parents for not funding the extravagant school break vacations he had wanted as a kid, that while the four of us were having dinner at one of Chicago's most posh restaurants, an argument between them escalated to fisticuffs while the mother stood in the middle of the room shrieking at the top of her lungs.

Then there was the banker who liked dressing up like the red Power Ranger because the outfit energized him, who wanted me to start wearing the pink Power Ranger outfit. Just for fun. See what kind of energy we could create together.

There was the sales rep who, when I finally told him I no longer wanted to see him because he was too possessive sent the police to my apartment to retrieve all the gifts he'd ever given me plus a check for all the money he'd spent on dates.

I didn't care what Lillian thought. I knew Tony Jackson was a catch. Not that I was trying to catch anything for keeps. I just wanted to reel something in, try it out, then throw it back for the next fisherwoman's enjoyment.

Tony took my hand into his. "I like what I do. I'm happy. I meet interesting people." He stood and pulled me out of my seat. "In fact, I'm very happy." He led me into the crowd. I wondered if he moved as fluidly beneath the sheets as he did on the dance floor.

"Don't hurt me now," he said. I was a pretty good dancer, too. I knew how to move.

"Your phone," I said.

"What?" Tony leaned down to better hear me.

I pointed to his flashing cell phone. He looked at the number on the caller identification and stopped dancing.

"What's up?" he said into the receiver. He nodded several times then ordered the person on the other end to call nine-one-one.

"What's wrong?"

"My sister Brenda."

I had to take two steps to match a single stride of his. When we reached the street he pulled out a fifty dollar bill and handed it to me.

"What's this for?"

"Taxi."

I looked confused.

"I can't take you home. I have to get to Brenda's place. She's having some kind of episode."

# Chapter 14 – Maya

Brenda sat at the kitchen table, an oxygen mask covering her nose and mouth. Two paramedics packed up their gear as we burst into the room.

"Baby-girl, you all right?" Tony dropped to one knee in front of his sister. Tears instantly brimmed in her eyes.

He turned to the paramedics."What happened?"

"She hyperventilated," said the female paramedic, "couldn't catch her breath, that's all. She's fine. We just gave her a little oxygen."

I watched Tony's frame decompress.

"Thank God." He handed his sister a tissue. She blew her nose.

"Why not tell her to take a break until the baby comes?" added the other paramedic. "Forget about cleaning the house."

I noticed the mop and bucket in the corner of the kitchen.

"No problem." He extended his hand to the paramedic. "Thanks. I'll talk to her."

After the paramedics walked out of the room Tony turned to Brenda. "Have you lost your mind?"

The tears that swam in the corner of her eyes spilled down her cheeks. She rested her head on the table and sobbed. He wrapped his arms around her while her body shook from the force of her crying. I turned away from them. The moment seemed too intimate to watch. I felt like a voyeur.

"I dropped a jar of mustard." Her voice was still shaky with unshed tears. "I was just tying to clean it up."

"I understand," he soothed her. "Don't cry. I'm sorry for yelling at you."

"All of a sudden I couldn't breathe."

I felt the weight of unshed tears in my own eyes.

"I can't lose this baby. I can't lose Dean and the baby."

I walked out of the kitchen. My heart felt heavy with sorrow, not just for Brenda but for myself as well.

I sat on the sofa in the living room and watched as Tony stroked his sister's hair and wished I hadn't been an only child. I longed for a sibling. When she finally pulled back from his embrace I could tell she was startled when she noticed me sitting on the sofa in the living room. I stood and walked toward the kitchen. Tony beckoned for me to come in.

"I'm sorry," was the only thing I could think to say.

"No, I'm sorry." Tears threatened to spill from her eyes again."You were on a date and I fucked it up."

"Don't worry about it." I smiled at Tony."We have plenty of time for other dates."

This time he smiled."We do?"

"Yeah, we do."

# Chapter 15 – Maya

I wove the strands of Brenda's hair into corn rows. I could tell she was both surprised and impressed at my skill. "I haven't braided anyone's hair since my mother." I stopped myself before finishing the sentence.

"What?" She was watching my reflection in the mirror above the dresser in her bedroom where she sat wrapped in what I assumed was one of Dean's flannel shirts.

"Was in the hospital. She died a couple of years ago."

"You guys were close, huh?"

"It was always just the two of us. I never knew my dad." The motion of my hand slowed for a moment. I was surprised at the effortlessness with which I revealed to Brenda a piece of my history that I rarely discussed. "I always told mom I wanted an older brother and a younger sister. And she would say, well, all you have is me and that's all you're going to get."

I watched Brenda watching me in the mirror.

"I was sixteen when my mother died. I know she loved me but we seemed to spend all our time fussing at each other. I couldn't understand it then but now I do." She rubbed her swollen belly.

"This should last at least a couple of weeks," I said after I finished the last of the braids.

"Thank goodness, one less thing to do."

"Getting ready for a baby is a lot of work."

In the days before Deuce and Sandy came to visit I spent an afternoon looking at cribs and cradles and gliding rockers at a few of the baby super stores. I had never even heard of gliding rockers until I saw them on display at every place I went.

"I feel like a damned whale."

"Well, you look great. You're glowing."

"Gas."

I liked her. She and Tony were really cool people.

"I haven't seen my feet in over a month."

I wasn't sure what to say so I changed the subject. "I love the theme you picked for the baby."

She smiled. "Thanks. Dean and I didn't want pastel."

"Me either."

"You have kids?"

I quickly shook my head. I must be suffering from sleep deprivation. "No, I've never been married."

"You don't have to be married to have children."

"That was a stupid comment, huh?"

"You want to?"

"Want to what? I knew what she was talking about but I didn't feel comfortable with the direction the conversation had taken.

"Have kids? Get married?"

I shrugged noncommittally. "I don't know."

"Well, if you don't, who the hell does?"

## Chapter 16 – Maya

Tony pulled his car to a stop in front of my condo. We sat without speaking, watching as people moved up and down Michigan Avenue as if it were in the middle of the day and not the wee hours of the morning. The stubble of beard that had grown in over the past few hours made him look even more handsome, rugged.

"So are you going to answer my question?" He looked confused."What makes me so special? I asked you that in the club."

He reached for my hand. I allowed it to rest comfortably within his grip and leaned back in the passenger seat. I stared through the open sun roof at the stars dotting the night sky.

"I don't know," he began. "Something about you

makes me want to just, I don't know, reach out and take care of you."

"I can take care of myself." I extricated my hand from Tony and sat up.

"I know that you can. What you don't know is that I can, too."

He leaned closer to me and kissed me gently. It took a while for me to lower my guard and respond to the pressure of his lips against mine. I felt myself getting moist.

"And that needing someone isn't a sign of weakness."

The bulge in the front of his pants indicated he was feeling something, too. "Sorry I didn't get you home early."

"Life happens." I wanted to laugh at his attempts to covertly hide his erection.

"Want to come up for a few minutes?"

His smile illuminated the entire car but I bit my lips as soon as the words escaped. Tony was a complication I didn't need right now. He was a fish I wasn't sure I'd be able to toss back in the water after a brief sampling. Lillian was right. I should go to Jamaica and have a fling. Go somewhere where I wouldn't have to see the object of my temporary affection every day when I was through with him. Create my own version of *How Maya Got Her Groove Back*.

Tony raised my hand to his lips. "I want to, but not for just a few minutes." He pulled himself away from me. "I better let you go while I still have the willpower to leave."

"Can I see you tomorrow?"

"Tomorrow?"

"Yeah, the day after today?

I hesitated.

"Around seven o'clock? Will that give you enough time to make it home from work?"

I wanted to pull my gaze away from his but I felt trapped under a hypnotic spell.

"You like Thai? I know this place that has incredible take out."

Look away, the voice inside my head cautioned. As long as I stared into his eyes I would agree to anything. I gripped the door handle and opened it.

He leaned across my lap preventing me from opening the door any farther. I resisted the urge to rub my hands through his hair. Not until now had I noticed the faint beginnings of a bald spot at the top of his head; somehow that little imperfection made him even more attractive to me.

"So, it's a date?"

I nodded, then stepped out of the car. "Thanks, but you don't have to walk me up." I knew that I couldn't withstand a goodbye kiss at the door. I would embarrass myself by begging him to come upstairs.

He nodded and relaxed into his seat. "See you tomorrow then," he called through the open window.

I felt his eyes warming my backside as I walked into the building.

"Good morning, Miss Latimer," said the doorman.

"Good morning, Jeremy."

It wasn't until I was in the elevator cruising up to my condo that I realized I was humming. "Get a grip," I told myself. I had to get up in less than three hours but I didn't care. I still felt the glow of Tony's stare warming every part of my body.

## Chapter 17 – Maya

I walked into my boss's office. He looked serious. Butterflies fluttered in my gut. Perhaps the employee profiles I had presented had left him less than impressed.

"Close the door." As soon as it was shut, James said, "The management team at Musikiwa wants the Narcisco leadership team in Japan to make a presentation to their executive board before making a final decision on the acquisition."

"Just let me know what I need to do."

He handed me an airline ticket. "Flight to Tokyo leaves tonight at eight o'clock."

"Tonight?"

"We can work on the presentation on the plane."

"But."

He propped his feet on the desk. "But what?" I could see that he was amused.

"I need to pack."

He nodded and smiled."We have a lot riding on this. You understand that, don't you?"

He walked around the desk and massaged my shoulders. My eyes widened in surprise. I wasn't sure what to do or say.

"You're so tense."

I stepped away from him. "Mr. Caplin, please."

He cut me off before I completed the rest of the sentence. "I didn't mean to offend you."

"No problem. None taken." I knew that was the correct response even though I didn't mean it. I was offended. Who did he think he was? He had no right to put his hands on me.

"Believe me, offending you is the last thing I want to do to you."

The double meaning hung in the air like laundry flapping in the breeze.

# Chapter 18 – Tony

I stood in the lobby as the doorman rang the buzzer to Maya's condo a third and final time.

"Hey, brother, it ain't my business, but man-to-man, she took a limo to the airport late this afternoon."

"Maya Latimer? Good looking chocolate brown sister with wavy hair?"

"For sho', I know who she is."

"We had a date."

The doorman shrugged.

I stepped back onto the street and punched in the phone number to her condo. I smiled when I heard her voice until I realized it was a recording. I disconnected, then dialed her office number. Her voice sounded on the other end. "I'll be out of the country for the next several days and unable to access voicemail. Leave a message. I'll return your call upon my return."

"Out of the country?" I picked up my shopping bag of Thai food and walked back to my car.

## Chapter 19 – Tony

I set a bowl of noodles in front of Brenda and fixed a plate for myself. "Shit happens," I said.

"I understand shit happens." Brenda raised a chuck of spiced chicken to her mouth."All I'm saying is what about a phone call? You guys had plans. Can't a brother get a phone call before the woman he's dating leaves the fuckin' country?"

"Give her a break." I had been involved with enough professional sisters to know that sometimes things happened that really were out of their control. But with an international flight she'd had at least of a couple hours waiting around the airport.

"Give yourself a break for a change." Brenda dug into the carton for more noodles. "It's about respect. Not to mention good old fashioned home training.

Maya's nice enough but she ain't looking to set up housekeeping no time soon. Trust me."

I sighed and shrugged. I wasn't sure.

# Chapter 20 – Maya

I read the card on the bouquet of yellow roses for the third time. *Still looking forward to our second date,* signed Tony.

"Someone has a secret admirer," teased my assistant Maggie.

I hadn't even thought about Tony until I was winging my way over the ocean in route to Tokyo. By then it was too late to call. James sat across from me during the entire flight and I didn't want to open the door for a discussion of my personal life. And as soon as the plane landed there was a whirlwind of activity with the Musikiwa executives.

I looked up in response to the knock on my office door. From the other side of the glass Maggie watched intently as I beckoned for Tony to enter and close the door.

"Welcome back."

*Surrender to Love*

"I'm so sorry."

He held up his hand to stop me.

I started again. "Thank you for the flowers."

"You're very welcome."

I felt guilty he had spent so much money on them. I wasn't really a big flower person and I could tell these weren't the roses vendors sold at the top of the entrance ramps off the freeway. He had spent some loot on them. But as Donna informed me when I called to tell her that Tony had sent me flowers, UPS drivers make good money.

"If he really doesn't have any kids and he's not a player out there dating everything with a coochie, he's probably got more disposable cash than you," she had said.

"No need to apologize," he said. "Just be ready at eight o'clock tonight."

I started to protest.

"You know how long I waited for you? Bag of take-out in hand?"

"Okay, I'll be ready."

"What should I wear?"

He smiled and licked his lips. "Something funky."

# Chapter 21 – Maya

House music banged through the stereo speakers as Tony cruised through neighborhoods that grew increasingly dilapidated as the pigmentation of the inhabitants grew deeper. I wondered where we were going but didn't ask. I didn't really care.

"How was Japan?" he asked me.

"Good." I really felt relaxed with him.

"A couple of years ago I went to Beijing and Shanghai."

"Really?" I hoped he wasn't offended by my surprise. I hated it when people put me in a box. What? UPS drivers couldn't have passports? Maybe I was more like Lillian than I realized.

"Yeah, I wanted to go somewhere where I would

*Surrender to Love*

know I was really far from home."

I tried to identify the feeling I had when I was with him. Safe. I think that was it. Safe.

"I know what you mean. When you're in Europe or even Australia, until people open their mouths you could be in any major metropolitan area.

"Exactly. White folks are white folks."

That's what it was. Safe. I knew that for whatever time we were together, if something happened, he could handle it. I could let down my guard for a little while. I could relax.

After we passed what seemed like the thirteenth beauty supply store, I couldn't resist any longer. "Where are you taking me?"

"We're here." He pulled into the parking lot of a run down skating rink. The bulbs in three of the letters had blown out.

"Where is here?"

"Come on." He extended his hand and helped me out of the car. "You said you grew up on the south side, right?"

I nodded.

"Then I know you can skate. When Brenda was in high school I thought I was going to have to torch this place to keep her behind from hanging out here all the time."

"Sorry to disappoint you but I don't." No need going into the diatribe explaining that the only places I was allowed to go when I was a kid was school and straight home.

"Then I'll teach you." He pushed through the front doors of the building. Loud hip-hop music pounded over the loud speakers. Strobe lights flashed in the darkened room as skaters crowded the wooden arena. A group of teenage boys hung around the perimeter watching the door. They waved and shouted to Tony as we entered. Each boy fell silent when they realized Tony and I were together.

"Hey fellas," he called the boys over. "I'd like you to meet a friend of mine, Maya Latimer."

A chorus of "What's up? Hey, hi, and what's happening" ensued.

"So you're just going to stand around? Or we're going to skate?"

The boys mobilized into action and joined the other teenagers on the crowded skating rink floor. I watched them, not sure if I was most impressed by the boys or Tony. The man knew how to move his body.

"They're good," I said when Tony rolled over to the bench where I was sitting.

He held out a pair of skates to me. "Size six?"

I nodded. He kneeled in front of me and laced them up, "Too tight?"

I shook my head. "Perfect."

"When Brenda's husband shipped off last year I promised him I'd fill in for him with his boys until he got home."

He helped me stand up. "He and a babe he went to high school with started the North Avenue Project."

"I never heard of it." I took a few tentative steps.

"It's really just a shoe-string operation, sort of shelter for women and after-school program for teenagers in the neighborhood. Gives the boys a safe place to hang out, shoot hoops, then every week or so we go somewhere." He smiled as I rolled around the rink without his assistance. "When we can get someone to donate the tickets, we go to a baseball or basketball game."

"That's really cool." I made a mental note to check our sky box schedule. These kids would probably get a real kick hanging out at a professional baseball game, even if the Cubs didn't win. Wrigley Field was a pretty neat stadium.

*My* first baseball game was compliments of Narcisco Industries and Cameron Williams, the only other professional black person in the Southwest region where I spent my first tour of duty when I joined Narcisco. Cameron had knocked on the wall outside my cubicle and laid two baseball play-off tickets on my desk. I was surprised by the butterflies that fluttered in my stomach. I had never noticed how attractive he was; square jaw, hazel eyes, dark brown hair. I wondered if he was mixed-race. Until that day I'd thought he was the type of brother who avoided sisters. Some black folks got off on being the only one.

But that wasn't true at all. In a lot of ways he was the male version of my friend Donna, super smart and pro-black to the tenth degree. Maybe that's why I was instantly drawn to her. She reminded me of Cameron. He was special. And the entire time we dated, he made me feel special. He was the person who started me wearing my hair natural. We'd been on vacation, our first trip together, my first visit to Barbados, the island of his father's birth.

"Not tonight," he said. He took the blow dryer I was preparing to use from my hands. "You don't need all that stuff." He indicated the arsenal of appliances and potions on the bathroom countertop whose mission it was to smooth away the natural waviness from my hair. "You look beautiful just the way you are."

I opened my mouth to protest but the way he looked at me caused the words to evaporate in my throat. He massaged gel into my hair and fluffed it around my face. "There." He stood back and observed his handiwork. "Look."

When I saw myself reflected through the eyes of the man standing next to me, I felt beautiful. When Cameron and I went to dinner on the last evening of our vacation and the Bajan people treated us like visiting royalty, I felt like a Nubian princess. And when I returned home and continued to wear my hair naturally and received daily complements, I continued to feel pretty.

So when I called my mother, I forgot to erect a shield that would protect me from things that were not beautiful. When I told her I wanted to bring my boyfriend home for the holidays and she asked, "Why?" I was struck dumb by the simplicity of the question. I wasn't sure what to say. Why? For the same reason families around the world gathered together at holiday time. Camaraderie? Tradition? Enjoyment of one another's company? Because that's what people do.

"I don't want to meet that nigger."

I inhaled deeply. "We're going to his folks' place for the New Year. We have to drive through Chicago, anyway."

"Don't do me no favors."

"Mommy, I didn't mean it like that. Of course I *want* to spend Christmas with you. I've spent every Christmas of my life with you. That's why I saved my vacation so we could come to Chicago and go to St. Louis."

"How long you taking off?"

"Two weeks."

"Two weeks? Girl, don't mess around and let that nigger get you fired. You know these men, especially black ones, just looking for a girl like you, making good money with no sense when it comes to men."

I didn't bother to tell her as a sales rep Cameron made more than I did as a human resources manager. She wouldn't believe me. She'd think I was making excuses for him.

"Maybe his parents got a big house but you know I live in this little apartment. There ain't no room for a man."

"But mom he's already told his family. We're already making plans."

I heard my mother sigh. "When you going to learn your lesson? What that man want don't mean nothing to me and it shouldn't mean nothing to you. You going to be a fool your whole life?"

"Mom, please."

"Look, I ain't telling you what to do. You're grown. Go spend Christmas *and* New Year's with his family.

I've been alone all my life. I know how to be alone."

"Mama, I want to be with you."

"I told you, don't do me no favors."

"All right, mommy."

"All right what?"

"I'll tell Cameron it's not convenient for him to come home with me. I can probably still get a flight but I won't be able to make it until Christmas Eve or early Christmas Day." I wouldn't completely kowtow to her extortion.

"Whatever you want to do, baby. Whenever you get here I'll have a sweet potato pie waiting for you. You still like sweet potato pie, don't you?"

"Yes."

"I was going to make ham and turkey with that sausage stuffing. You still eat pork?"

"Yes, I still eat pork."

"Well you know hanging around with all them crazy white folks you never know. You eating sushi?"

"Sometimes."

"Girl, you couldn't pay me all the money in the world to eat raw fish."

"Look, I'll give you a call when I get all my flight information." I wanted to hang up before she realized I was crying.

"Okay then, remember mommy loves you."

"Love you too."

I placed the receiver back in the cradle.

So when Cameron came over with a collection of maps and brochures for B&Bs so we could route our trip, I didn't know how to tell the man I had fallen in love with that he wasn't welcome in my mother's home. So since I didn't know how to say that, I lied. I told him the company had rescinded my time off.

"But I thought it was all set?"

"I thought so, too, but duty calls."

He wrapped me in his arms."Well, we could go to one of those places where you cut down your own

Christmas tree, decorate it." He sipped a mug of hot chocolate laced with Bailey's Irish Cream. "It'll be fun spending our first holiday together, just the two of us."

"But your parents are expecting you."

"They'll be disappointed but they'll understand." He pulled me to his chest. "My folks were really looking forward to meeting you. You're the first girl I've ever brought home to meet the family. My mom and Aunt Boot were preparing the inquisition."

I pulled away from him because I didn't know how to tell him I couldn't spend the holidays with him because *I* was going home, alone. So that night when he wanted to make love, I accused him of treating me like a whore. And when he proclaimed his love, I told him that things were moving too fast. And when I woke up with a box from Tiffany's lying on the pillow next to me, I panicked and said I didn't want to see him anymore.

As I rolled around the dilapidated skating rink I realized that not since Cameron had I felt the way I was feeling with Tony. Safe. And beautiful. And desired. I clutched him to steady myself. The strength of his arms around my waist felt comforting.

"Dean was a really good guy. I miss him," he was saying.

"I'm really sorry I won't ever get to meet him."

"Yeah, he was a good friend. He would have made a great dad."

"You will, too." I was pleased that I was actually moving in time with the music.

"You're making me an offer?"

Before I answered, Tony wrapped his arms around my waist and skated us into the middle of the crowd. We moved in unison on the floor."All right now," he teased when I was able to keep pace with him. He let go of my waist and spun around clapping his hands. I reached out to grab his outstretched fingers but lost my balance. I landed with a thud on the skating rink floor. The other skaters moved around us without missing a beat.

"You okay?"

As he pulled me up we started laughing. "Is this any way to treat a lady?" I brushed off the seat of my pants.

"My bad. Sure you're okay?"

I nodded. An old school slow jam played over the loud speakers. He wrapped his arms around me once again.

"I promise I won't let you fall." We skated with the crowd that seemed to move like a single organism. I saw his boys watching us from the sidelines. Tony signaled for them to ask one of the girls hugging the wall to skate. Each boy shook his head. Though they feigned disinterest I knew it was fear of rejection that kept them from interacting with their female counterparts.

"Maybe you could teach a little session for the boys on how to talk to girls," he whispered in my ear as we twirled around the wooden floor.

"Maybe you should teach them. You're pretty smooth."

"You know what I mean." He hugged me more closely to his chest. As though he were a puppet master pulling an invisible string, my head tilted backward to receive the kiss he planted gently on my lips.

"All right, Mr. T." The teenagers jeered from the sidelines.

The slow song ended."Want to take a break? I need to spend a little more time with the fellas."

I nodded. "Hey," I called out as he skated away from me, "Why don't you come by for dinner tomorrow night? About eight o'clock? I owe you."

"You're not going to stand me up, are you?"

"No way."

# Chapter 22 – Maya

Donna smirked. "What happened to *I'm going to just hit it and forget it*?"

"That's still the plan." I averted my eyes from her gaze and searched under a lettuce leaf for another piece of chicken.

"Don't sound that way to me." She opened a package of wet wipes and cleaned her fingers of hot wing sauce.

"Just shut up and order desert."

"I ain't mad at you." She perused the desert menu."Whatever you want to do, if it's good for you and to you, go for it, girlfriend. Forget what anybody else has to say, even me."

"It's just that Tony seems different."

Donna looked over the top of her menu at me.

*Surrender to Love*

"I think my girl's got a case of puppy love."

I waved the waiter away. "I think it's just that I've finally figured it out."

"Figured what out?"

"Where I've been making my mistake in the past."

"What? You think you shouldn't be in human resources? I can see that."

"No, not on the work front. With men."

Donna set down her menu.

"I've always picked corporate brothers. You know what I mean?"

She nodded.

"I had to have a man who made as much money as me. If I had the initiative to get an advanced degree, I had to have a man who had done the same. If I could afford a half a million dollar home, he better have one worth seven fifty."

"Ain't nothing wrong with that. You got the right to want what you want."

"But maybe I just need a nice working-class guy."

"A nice working-class guy?" She repeated the words slowly.

"Yeah, an average Joe."

She took off her reading glasses.

"What? You disagree?"

"It's not that."

"You're not turning into Lillian on me, are you?" I thought Donna would understand where I was coming from.

"Girlfriend, life is not a video game." She sounded like Tony when he was talking to one of the teenagers at the skating rink.

"What are you talking about?"

"You can't go to a level and select the type of man you want, plop him down and think he'll act the way you program him to act.

"I know that."

"Do you?" She shrugged. "I've always said you were smarter than me."

"What's that supposed to mean?"

"It took me almost two decades of marriage before I learned that lesson." She held out her hand. I grasped her outstretched fingers."All you can expect from a man is a relationship with the person that he is."

She raised her hand to stop me from speaking. "Listen to what I'm saying to you, girlfriend."

I nodded my assurance that I would remain quiet.

"All you get is a man. The man who he is, not who you want him to be or who you thought he was. You feel me?"

I nodded.

"Not who you wished he'd allow himself to be if only he would ... fill in the blank ... go back to school, stop drinking, stop smoking bud, start exercising, get a better job ... doesn't matter, all you get is him."

She let go of my hand and beckoned for the waitress to come take her order. I sat there quietly allowing myself to absorb what she'd just said. I felt her. I really did.

# Chapter 23 – Maya

James beckoned for me to come into his office. "I just got off the phone with our contact in Japan," he said as soon as I walked in. My heart thumped as I replayed the presentation I'd made over again in my head.

"You really wowed them when we were there."

"Thanks." I sighed in relief.

He got up from his desk and came to stand beside me. My eye's narrowed like a cat's when he rubbed his forefinger along the side of my cheek.

"You're a beautiful woman." His voice was so soft I wondered if I had misunderstood him. Perhaps, in a different setting I would have been flattered. Though I hadn't crossed the color line I had contemplated it. I

*Surrender to Love*

think every successful single black woman in America has at least thought on it. And it seemed like more and more of us were doing more than thinking about it. A day rarely passed when I didn't see a white-man, black-woman coupling.

"Do it," Lillian had challenged the last time we talked about whether I should or shouldn't. "You meet more white men at your level than you do black. Men like Rick are far and few in between."

"I can't believe you," I shot back. She laughed. "I'm saying it's okay for you to cross the line," she corrected. "Me? I tried it once and couldn't take it."

"Why not?" I laughed. I knew that Lillian was about to say something outrageous.

She held up two fingers. "One, his pink toes; two, his little pink dick."

"Was it really small?"

"I can't speak for all white men. I've only been with one and I was only with him once."

"All right," I said, "Now that you have the politically correct disclaimer on the table, was it?"

She looked around the room as if she were searching for hidden spies before she held her thumb and forefinger about an inch apart.

"No."

"Yes."

"Really?"

"Really, girl."

This time I looked around before I asked my next question. Lillian leaned forward to better hear me. "What about going downtown?"

"You mean could he eat pussy?"

She rolled her neck in sister girl fashion. "Boyfriend was terrible."

"No," I screamed.

"Can you believe that?"

There was another myth I would have to put to rest

along with the tooth fairy and Santa Claus. But somehow, as I looked at my boss I had a feeling an experience with him would be different than Lillian's white-guy encounter. He wasn't a bad looking man. His body was lean and well-muscled. In a different place and time, maybe his attentions might be welcomed but right now, in his office, his compliment lingered like the smell of three-day old fish.

"Thank you." I decided not to make a big deal of the moment. De-escalate conflict. That was my strategy. Unless he touches me, then I would have to go serious south-side-sister-girl on his ass. I could still reconnect with my roots when need be. At least that's what I told myself.

James sat down and propped his feet on top of his desk. "Do you know what I've always heard?" He placed his interlaced fingers behind his head. "That once you go black you never come back."

"So the saying goes," I responded without emotion. If he was looking for a reaction from me I refused to give it to him. Of course, I could never tell Donna he said some shit like that. Girlfriend would organize so many protests against his racist-sexist behavior all our heads would be spinning.

He took his feet from the desk, his demeanor all business again. "Do you know the number one key to success?"

This man must be bipolar. His moods swung from one extreme to the next. "I'm not good at guessing games. Tell me."

"Being willing to do what's necessary."

I pondered the spoken and unspoken meaning to what he had just said but made no comment. He took a stack of papers from his desk and handed them to me.

"I need you to prepare a presentation for tomorrow's meeting on Musikiwa Industries. No more than twenty to twenty-five slides."

I glanced at the Rolex on my wrist before I responded, "I'll have it for you first thing in the morning." I reached for the papers.

"No," said James. "I need it before you leave. Tonight."

"How early do you need it? Six?" I raised my eyebrows. He stared at me, his face immobile. "Five?" I countered.

"Before you leave. Tonight."

I took a deep breath. I knew this was a power play and we both knew who held the power. I nodded and walked out of his office.

# Chapter 24 – Maya

I glanced at my watch and pushed my grocery cart through the produce section a little more quickly. I threw a bag of pre-washed European salad greens, plum tomatoes still on the vine, scallions and cucumbers into the cart then wheeled myself into the meat section. "Crap," I said when I looked at my watch again. It was already fifteen minutes past seven. This wasn't going to work.

I did a u-turn and pushed my cart to the gourmet pre-packaged food aisle. Now we're talking. I debated between the lobster, which I rejected because I didn't want him to think I was trying to impress him, and the prime rib, which I rejected because I wasn't sure if he ate red meat. I selected chicken cordon bleu because every black man I knew liked chicken.

Five minutes before Tony arrived I poured the salad

*Surrender to Love*

fixings into a bowl and stuffed the empty containers in the garbage. I looked around the kitchen to make sure no evidence remained that I hadn't prepared the meal with my very own hands.

"Coming," I called when the doorbell rang.

Tony walked into the condo with two bottles of chilled wine. "Chardonnay," he said as he handed the bottles to me."Very dry the way my lady likes it."

I made a mental note to give him Brownie points for remembering my drink preference. I led him to the dining room table. "Hungry?"

"Starving. I've been thinking about you all day rattling pots and pans for me. I know a lot of career women don't cook these days." He sat down. Soft music flowed through the room like an ocean breeze.

I picked at my food. I hadn't felt like this since my seventh grade crush on Kevin Simpson. I pushed my chicken from one side to the other side of my plate as I watched him devour the meal I had placed on my good china, dishes I'd purchased new, a simple English bone china pattern trimmed in platinum. I didn't mind spending money on the things I wanted. I wasn't going to deny myself hoping somebody would give them to me one day as a wedding gift. What if I never got married? Which at this point in my life was a likely scenario.

Tony pushed back his plate and sighed. "That was great."

"Thanks."

"I love the take-out section at Trader Joe's. It's incredible."

I pushed back from the table so quickly, if not for his quick reflexes, the chair would have slammed to the floor. I couldn't believe how angry I felt. "Look, I work all day." I picked up my plate and started for the kitchen. Tears welled up in my eyes.

In an instant, Tony was beside me. He took the plate from my hand and placed it on the kitchen counter. "Hey, wait a minute, that wasn't meant to be a slam."

I stood still and willed the tears not to fall from my eyes. I didn't know what was wrong with me. My period had ended last week so it wasn't that time of the month. Maybe I was just feeling the effects of too little sleep and too much work.

As if approaching a frightened animal he didn't want to bolt, Tony moved slowly toward me. He gently wrapped me in his arms and spoke softly in my ear. "Babe, I know you work hard. I'm not complaining. That wasn't a criticism."

I looked up at him. In my entire dating life, it seemed that I had never gotten it right. Maybe my mother was wrong. Men weren't the problem. It was me.

"Everything's okay. Hear me?"

"I wanted to cook for you. Honest I did." Even to my own ears I sounded like a ten year old making excuses for not cleaning her room.

He pressed his finger against my lips and shook his head. "Babe, you don't have to explain. This," he said, making a sweeping gesture with his arms, "Has been wonderful. I don't need my woman acting like my personal slave to boost my ego. I'm proud of you and everything you do. Ain't nothing like a strong black woman."

I relaxed into his chest. "I know I don't have the right to complain but sometimes I just feel so damned tired."

"You have a right to be tired. You work hard."

"I do." It felt great to hear his acknowledgement of the demands of my schedule.

"You're at work before I get there."

That's right. And even when I got home, even if I didn't open my briefcase and tackle the piles of work I had in there, I was thinking about work. Thinking about what I ought to be doing or fretting over whether what I'd done was good enough.

"I start work at six but I'm done at two, and when

*Surrender to Love*

I'm done, I'm done."

I pushed away from him so that I could look into his eyes."All I ever do is work."

"We're going to have to change that."

"But I realize I'm blessed. Not many people, much less black women, are living the life I have."

"Got to take the bitter with the sweet."

Only when I stopped moving did I realize Tony and I had been swaying together to the music.

"What's wrong?"

"That's what my mother used to say all the time. Even when we found out the cancer had returned after three months of chemo."

"I'm sorry." He hugged me more tightly. "I'll take the bitter for you. You deserve nothing but sweetness."

Deuce never said things like that to me. I felt my breasts pressed against his chest. When I looked into his eyes again, it was evident he wanted me as much as I wanted him. Without speaking, I led him into my bedroom. Candles illuminated the room with a soft, flickering light.

As I lay on my back I wondered how I had become almost naked. I had no recollection of removing my clothes. My thoughts were consumed with the feel of his hands on my bare flesh, the smell of his cologne.

"Take that off," I commanded.

In a single motion, he took off his undershirt and flung it onto the floor. I leaned up on my elbows. He unhooked my bra.

"Perfect," he said as my breasts sprang forward like two puppies who wanted to play. He squeezed them softly. When his tongue flickered over the hardened areoles I hoped my groaning hadn't sounded as loud to him as it had to me.

"I want to feel you inside me," I said. *La petit mort*. I understood why the French called an orgasm the little death because if he didn't fill me with himself I would die. I would absolutely die.

He shook his head and resisted my efforts to direct his penis into me. "I don't want to rush things," he whispered.

"Make this one quick, then we have the rest of the night, don't we?"

He nodded and opened the drawer in the night stand where I pointed. "Always got to be in charge, huh?" he teased me.

I ripped open the condom wrapper and said a little prayer of thanks that I had more. I had almost thrown away the package when I began my self-imposed celibacy. But when the sun rose, I realized a three-pack may have been enough for me and Deuce but not for Tony and me. "Note to self," I said out loud as I lay flat on my back, "Buy more condoms." I sat up on the edge of the bed, satiated. Every part of my body felt alive and vibrant.

"Where you going?" He rolled over and wrapped his arms around my waist.

I looked down at my toes glad that my pedicure still looked fresh. Good girl for not letting your personal hygiene slip. Not that I think he would have cared one way or the other if my toenails had paint chips.

He pulled me back down and wrapped his arms around me.

"Today's a big day," I explained as I extricated myself from his embrace.

He sat up and nuzzled my neck. "Call in sick."

I rubbed my hand along his face. "I wish I could." I would be perfectly content to spend the entire day snuggled in bed with him. "But I can't."

He released me from his grasp. "Okay," he said. "Last one in the shower is a rotten egg." He jumped out of bed.

"Hey," I cried and ran after him.

# Chapter 25 – Maya

I typed furiously at my computer.

"Hey, babe."

I hadn't noticed that Tony had come into my office until he set a bouquet of flowers on my desk. I automatically lifted my face toward him to receive his kiss. "When did you have time to get these?" I pushed my nose deep into the bouquet. When I looked up James Caplin stood in my doorway.

"Excuse me," he said walking into my office.

I wondered if he had seen Tony kiss me.

"I never realized we got such personal attention from UPS. No wonder FedEx is losing market share."

I guess he had. "Mr. Caplin." I jumped up. "I'm sorry."

"I just wanted to inform you in person that in a stock

trade that was consummated at eight ten this morning Musikiwa International acquired Narcisco Industries."

I plopped back down into my seat. "Oh my God, the deal went through."

"And once you're done making out with the delivery man I'll fill you in on the details." My boss turned to walk out.

"Hey," said Tony in a tone that demanded attention.

James stopped and turned to face him.

"I know you're the big-boss man but watch the tone you use when you talk to my woman."

"Your woman?" James looked from Tony to me. I dropped my gaze to the floor. Without responding he walked out of the office and shut the door.

"I've always heard he was an asshole," said Tony. "But this is my first time experiencing it first hand."

I glared at him.

"What?" He shrugged, his brow wrinkled.

"What is wrong with you?"

"What's wrong with me?"

"That's my boss."

"I know who he is. I've been around here longer than you, remember?"

"My boss, the man that I report to, the person who determines my future." I enunciated each word slowly and articulately.

"I don't care who he is. Nobody talks to you like that, at least not when I'm around. What kind of man would I be if I let that disrespect stand?"

I turned around and stared out of my window at the view of Lake Michigan. I inhaled deeply and tried to regulate my breath. When I turned back to him I was able to speak in a normal tone. "So this is some kind of macho-man bullshit?"

"What do you mean by this?" The vein in the front of his forehead pulsated but his voice remained low.

I took a deep breath. "Since you have so much tenure

here answer me this." I tried not to raise my voice either. Maggie was no longer pretending that she wasn't watching us. I knew this little episode would be spread all over the building before lunch.

"How many other black female vice presidents work here?"

"What's your point?"

"How many have you ever seen working here?" I demanded. "I want a number."

It took several seconds before Tony responded. Finally he said, "None."

I nodded. "Right. None. So do you know how hard it is being the *only* one? Especially the *first* one? To command respect around here?"

He didn't respond.

"Now I have to deal with this shit."

"What *shit* is that?" His tone was so cold it startled me but I wouldn't back down.

"That every time my boss looks at me he'll think about me fucking the UPS man."

As soon as the words left my mouth I knew that I had gone too far. His features seemed to transform to stone. "I didn't realize that's what you were doing." He barely spoke above a whisper.

"Come on Tony, you know I didn't mean it like that."

"I guess I'm not as smart as you because I don't know that."

"Tony, stop it. I'm sorry."

"Okay, tell me. How did you mean it?"

I hesitated as I searched for the right words. "I meant," I began, picking my words carefully, "That I need to keep my personal and my professional life separate."

"Who doesn't? You think I got babes riding in the truck next to me?"

"You know what I mean."

"Keep our thing on the down-low? Is that it?"

"Yeah, you understand, right? Nothing personal,

just business."

He shook his head. "I see," he said slowly. "You meant it like *that*."

"You understand, right?"

"Yeah, babe, I understand. But I don't roll like that."

I stood in front of him and tried to take his hand into mine but he pulled away. "No, somebody might walk in."

"Tony, come on? Don't be this way."

"You need to find yourself another stud service, baby-girl. I'm looking for more than just a good fuck."

I had never heard him use foul language before. The word sounded especially vulgar coming from his lips.

"And you were very good," he added. "If you want to switch to a different kind of prostitution you've got a bright future there too." He walked out of my office before I gathered my thoughts enough to respond.

Maggie immediately popped her head inside my office door. "You okay?"

"I'm fine."

"Did you hear? We've been sold."

"Yeah," I said without enthusiasm.

"Mr. Caplin said to give you this." She held out a large white envelope.

"Thanks." I ripped open the package and removed a letter signed by the President of Musikiwa International. *Thank you for your valuable contribution. Congratulations, you have been awarded one hundred thousand shares of stock in Musikiwa International.*

I reread the letter three times.

"I see you've opened the letter."

James stood in my office doorway.

My neck snapped up. "Mr. Caplin," I began, "James," I corrected myself.

He waved his hand in dismissal. "Have you checked the stock price today?"

"No." I shook my head.

"Ninety-five and change and still climbing. The market loves this acquisition."

I calculated the value of the stock I had been awarded. I stopped, unable to speak when I came up with the number.

"Remember what I told you?"

My head was spinning.

"Take care of me. I take care of you."

# Chapter 26 – Tony

For a change Brenda sat quietly in the passenger seat as I pulled into the parking lot at Target. I knew she probably wanted to say I told you so but practiced restraint. Maybe motherhood does make women more empathetic. "There are a couple of things I want to pick up for my niece," I said.

"We don't need nothing," she began.

"This is between me and my niece." I emphasized the word *my*. At the rate my love life was progressing, being an uncle might be the closest I was going to get to having children in my life. Brenda tapped my arm and motioned for me to stop pushing the cart as we strolled through the baby aisle.

"What?"

*Surrender to Love*

She squeezed my arm and tilted her head to the right.

I peered around her and saw a tall African-American woman looking through the clearance rack of boy's clothing. Her long dread-locks were tied back with a Kente-inspired scarf. The pants of her postal uniform showed that she had just the right amount of junk in her trunk.

"I don't see a ring," whispered Brenda.

"You women have spyware implants? How can you tell that from way over here?" I noticed Brenda still wore her wedding band but I made no comment.

Brenda tried to nudge the cart toward the woman but I restrained her. "I don't need you to quarterback my love life," I whispered.

"Yes, you do."

"No I don't."

"She's pretty. And you know the post office pays good money, so girlfriend can take care of herself."

The woman placed two outfits in her cart.

"Looks like she's got a kid. That's good. You like kids," she informed me as if I were suffering from dementia and it was her responsibility to remind me of tidbits I had forgotten about myself.

I gave my sister a withering look as the woman rolled her cart toward us. I dared her to say something, but if I had put money down I would have lost the bet. I should know better than to wager against my sister when she was on a matchmaking mission.

"Ain't it good to have a big brother willing to help his baby sister out?" Brenda called to the woman when they were in speaking distance.

The woman smiled and stopped her cart next to me. "It's always good to have a brother around," she answered Brenda then turned to me and smiled. Her teeth were straight and white. I did love a woman with a pretty smile.

"This is my big brother, Tony."

The woman's smile broadened. "Nice to meet you Brother Tony, I'm Sheila." She extended her hand.

"Nice to meet you, too," I said. After I released her hand, the woman waited to see if I would say more. I didn't. She looked in our shopping cart that had about a half dozen items in it.

"Even before I got divorced three years ago I couldn't get my husband to come shopping. Your brother seems to be doing a pretty good job at it." Though she addressed Brenda, the message was obviously intended to let me know she was available.

When they both concluded I wasn't going to strike up a conversation, the woman looked at Brenda who shrugged as if to say, *you know how retarded men can be.*

"Well, nice meeting you both. Congratulations on that baby," she said to Brenda."And hopefully, I'll see you again one day, Brother Tony."

I nodded in acknowledgement but said nothing.

"You're hopeless," Brenda said. She shook her head and took over the duty of pushing the shopping cart. I followed behind her. She was probably right.

# Chapter 27 – Maya

For the third time since Tony had left my office that morning I dialed his cell. I wasn't sure what I wanted to say but I knew I didn't want to leave things the way they were. I felt awful. At the end of his voice mail message, I opened my mouth to speak but no words came out. I had already left a message asking him to call me. Well, forget it. If this is how he wanted it, then forget him. Hit it and forget it. That really was the only way to go.

I looked through my glass wall at all the other empty offices. Everyone was probably at the celebration party Maggie had organized. They'd been celebrating the acquisition all day. That's where I needed to be. It wasn't often an announcement like this made employees and investors happy but that's what the Musikiwa

International-Narcisco Industries merger achieved. Like peanut butter and jelly, Siegfried and Roy, Sylvester and Tweety, we were meant to be together.

My heart pounded when my cell phone rang. On the first ring, I picked up the phone without checking the caller I.D. When Maggie's voice sounded on the other end of the line, I sighed. "Of course I'm coming over," I assured her. Tony wasn't going to call. I might as well accept it. Even Narcisco Industries had found a soulmate before me.

## Chapter 28 – Maya

I walked across the marbled entryway of the Chicago Sheraton and Towers Hotel, the official hotel of Narcisco Industries and now Musikiwa International. I wasn't in the mood to party but I knew I had to show my face.

"Maya?"

I turned toward a black woman in a hotel maid's uniform.

"Maya, girl, is that you? It's me, your Cousin Lottie."

"Cousin Lottie?"

Lottie took a tentative step toward me. I quickly closed the space between us and wrapped her in a warm embrace. I felt the sharp outline of her shoulderblades beneath her uniform. I hadn't seen her since my mother's funeral.

"I was on my way out and forgot my purse. If I

hadn't made a second trip I would have missed you. Ain't God good?" Lottie smiled. "Thank you, Jesus."

"You work here?" Duh, I thought after the words came out of my mouth.

"Yes ma-am, been here almost a year now."

I could tell she was proud of that achievement. She had a right to be. It was an accomplishment that had taken her a lifetime to claim. Other than an occasional stint doing day-work I never knew her to have a job.

"So you're off work?" I confirmed. I didn't want to be the reason she slipped up.

"Thank goodness. These white folks work you like a slave 'round here. But thank you Lord for waking me up and giving me the strength to make it through another day."

"Come on." I grabbed Lottie's hand and headed toward the hotel bar.

She pulled back. "They don't like us going in there."

"As much money as my company is spending here tonight, we'll go where ever we damned well please."

She cackled like one of the witches from William Shakespeare's play, *Macbeth*. "I heard that. I always knew you was going to be running shit one day. Yes, Jesus."

We settled into a corner booth. I sipped a glass of wine while Lottie nursed a tall glass of orange juice. My mother would never believe her cousin had turned down an offer of free booze. As if reading my mind, she said, "I don't drink no more. Haven't since right after your momma died. That really tore me up. Let me know I needed to get my shit together. Thank you Lord for sharing your light and your grace with me."

I assumed a new found commitment to Christianity must figure prominently in her ability to turn her life around. In our brief time together she'd invoked the name of the Lord more times than I could remember.

"I know your mama, rest her soul, thought I was going to be a drunk all my life but people can change, you know? Yes, Lord. Thank you Jesus." Lottie looked at me and shook her head. "Damn, you look just like your mama," she said as she stared at me.

"Thanks." I thought my mother was beautiful.

"I sure do miss her." Lottie sipped her drink. "But she's resting in the bosom of Jesus. Thank you Lord."

I observed my cousin over the rim of my glass. The years had been surprisingly kind to her. Her skin was smooth and unwrinkled. Black women were one of God's natural wonders. Though, too often, overlooked and under loved, we still looked good. Lottie was proof. She still weighed less than a hundred pounds but she had lost that gaunt, unhealthy look I associated with her.

Until I was about thirteen, for as far back as I could remember, at least half a dozen times a year, my mother dispatched herself, with me in tow, on a mission of mercy to Lottie's latest abode, a home she generally shared with her latest "boyfriend," and a few of her children. Sometimes, Lottie acknowledged our arrival with thanks but usually by the time we got there, the violence had ended, the boyfriend was gone and Lottie was sleeping it off on the couch.

My mother would do whatever necessary to restore our cousin's modesty; clean the blood from her nose and lips, put ice on a blackened eye, close her legs, pull down her skirt, refasten her brassiere. If Lottie could be roused from her drunken slumber, my mother forced her to eat something, usually a can of soup that we'd brought from our house, saved for just such an occasion. But as I grew older my mother and Lottie seemed to drift apart. Even when we knew that she was dying, she said she didn't want her cousin by her side. "Just call her when I'd dead."

"Are you sure?" I asked.

"Why would I want to see that drunk?" My mother had funny ways. And I learned it was best not to stir things up. Let sleeping dogs lie.

"It's hard to believe your mama used to be a hot cha-cha-cha. She got so mean and evil after her and your daddy broke up." Lottie was quiet for a few seconds. "I always thought she'd find somebody else but she just couldn't seem to shake him."

The movement of the room seemed to slow down. What had she said? "Who?" I asked. "Couldn't shake who?"

"Your daddy." Lottie looked at me suspiciously, as if she was wondering whether my mother's claims that I was so smart might have all been a lie. She swirled the juice in her glass, an old habit I assumed from the days when vodka would have also been in there. "Guess that's what happens when your heart gets broken and never gets fixed."

I set my wine down. I didn't want her to see my hand shaking. "What do you mean?"

"I used to think you looked like your daddy but now you look like your momma spit you out."

My heart pounded.

"'Cept for the hair. People used to think your daddy's hair was processed but it was naturally wavy. I had never seen a nigger black as your daddy with hair like that."

She seemed oblivious to the impact she was having on me.

"Damn, I used to wish I had your daddy's hair and your momma's legs."

Even pushing sixty my mother could stop construction crews when she walked by. I always thanked her for the long shapely legs with which I had also been blessed. Now, I knew to thank my father for my hair. I had gotten Lottie's wish, my father's hair and my mother's legs.

"Tiny Turner didn't have nothing on her."

I smiled and nodded.

"Mind if I smoke?"

I did, but I shook my head. If she had kicked the alcohol, she was entitled to hold onto one vice.

"These going to be next." She held up the pack of cigarettes. Of course she smoked the brand with the most tar and nicotine.

"You can do it," I encouraged.

"Yes, Lord, with the help of Jesus." She raised her hand in silent prayer.

"Your momma used to smoke 'til she found out she was pregnant with you. Then boom." She snapped her fingers. "She was done. Cold turkey." She took a long drag of her cigarette. "Your momma always was disciplined like that."

"My mother used to smoke?" I felt like I was watching an old Japanese horror film where the soundtrack and the picture weren't synchronized. I was on a time delay so it took several seconds for me to comprehend what Lottie was saying.

"Ain't that a bitch?"

Her new found religion may have cut her appetite for liquor but it had done nothing to rid her mouth of profanity.

"Ain't nothing worse than a reformed sinner." She blew the smoke from her cigarette away from my face, finished her orange juice and looked at her wrist watch. "You know I know all her shit." Lottie stressed the word, *all*.

I beckoned for the waiter to give us both a refill.

She chuckled.

"What?"

"You know your daddy used to sell weed?"

I shook my head. She didn't seem to realize I didn't know anything about my father. Now, it seemed I also knew little about my mother.

"That was one smooth talking son-of-bitch." She laughed. "And was as good looking as the day was long. He still is for his age."

My father was alive. And Lottie was in contact with him. Is that what I should surmise from that statement?

"Me and your momma used to package his shit up in sandwich bags. She'd be puttering her ass around the kitchen like she was June-fuckin'-Cleaver making lunch for the boys 'stead of nickel and dime bags of reefer."

"My mother?" I needed to clarify that she was still talking about my mother.

Lottie nodded. "Then Sonny would carry them around in your diaper bag. He sure loved yo' pretty little ass. Always wanted to take you with him. Wherever he was going. He'd have you all up and down Sixty-third Street."

A vague recollection of sitting on a bar stool sipping a drink with a paper umbrella and maraschino cherries danced at the edges of my memory.

Lottie lit another cigarette.

"But Lord have mercy your momma and your daddy used to fight like gamecocks. Fighting and fucking. That's all them two used to do." She chuckled again.

I couldn't imagine my mother passionate enough to fight or fuck. I asked, almost begged to know, "About what? What did they fight about?"

"About everything." She lowered her voice and looked around the darkened restaurant. "I shouldn't say this. Your momma would turn over in her grave if she heard me."

"What difference can it make now?" This is why my mother stopped Lottie from coming around when I got older. Lottie knew too much and once I was old enough and curious enough to ask questions she kept us apart.

Lottie sipped her drink. I had forgotten she had a flair for the dramatic. "One time your daddy gave your momma crabs. Lord, have mercy, she was hot. Wasn't but a few months after that she told me she was pregnant with you." She sighed. "I guess they made up, huh?"

"So what happened? Why'd they break up?" I wanted an answer to that question but more importantly I wanted to ask why had he deserted me? Just because he and my mother couldn't get along, what about me? What happened to his feelings for me?

Lottie shrugged. It seemed like she had lost the mood to talk. "Girl, I don't know." She shook her head. "I guess they was too much alike. Both of them head strong and stubborn." She shrugged again. "I think they really thought it could work. Sonny ain't never had no family. He was raised as a ward of the state which meant he raised himself up in the streets. I think he really liked the notion of having a little woman at home, baking biscuits from scratch and frying steak with gravy. Your momma knew she could cook, didn't she?"

"Yes, ma'am."

"Now, I can throw down, too. If there's one thing us country girls can do, it's cook." She shook her head. "But not like Sissy, 'specially pies. I never could get my crusts to be that light and flaky."

I couldn't remember the last time I'd had a good slice of sweet potato pie. I was going to bake one. I knew how. I just hadn't done it in a while.

Lottie swirled the contents of her glass again."And Lord knows he brought some excitement to that dull ass life of hers. She always had been a square. Quiet. Shy like, you know?"

I knew. I used to take my mother as my date to the fancy corporate affairs to which I was invited. I wanted to give her an opportunity to experience things she'd never done but after a few events, I stopped. Neither of us enjoyed it. My mother was uncomfortable and felt out of her element. I was a nervous wreck worrying about her whenever she was out of my sight. I'd usually find her sitting alone in a corner. She'd look so pathetic and I'd feel so guilty, I'd want to cry.

"I always told Sissy she was wrong to keep you two apart when you all had started out so close."

I beckoned for the waitress. "Can you bring a menu?" If I drank anything else without eating something I'd be

*Surrender to Love*

falling-down drunk. "What happened?" How had I gone from the apple of my father's eye to no contact at all? I took the menu from the waitress and quickly ordered. Lottie turned down my offer to buy her a meal.

"With all them low-life niggers hanging 'round the house all the time eventually something was bound to happen, you know what I'm saying?"

"No." I wasn't going to even pretend that I did.

"There was always a bunch of folks coming and going, mostly men, sometimes women. When your daddy wanted to get your momma riled up he'd tell her them women was his hoes. Claimed he was pimpin' them. Your momma pretended like she didn't care but she did. She was real jealous of him."

I debated whether to order something stronger than wine. I felt like I was going to need it.

"I never did trust that snaggle-tooth mother-fucker."

The waitress set a salad in front of me.

"Before your momma got sick I told her I had bumped into him. That's what she got mad at me about. 'Cause I recollected that time when old snaggled-tooth came to the house and she tried to pretend like the shit never happened." She leaned forward and spoke conspiratorially, "That's what broke 'em up."

Lottie took another cigarette from the pack. "I know what I know." She leaned forward again and stared directly into my eyes. "She could pretend like the shit never happened but I was there. I seen it, you know what I'm saying?"

I shook my head and beckoned for the waitress. I no longer felt buzzed or hungry. I was ready to go. I didn't want to hear anything else my cousin had to say. As Flavor Flav would say, "My time was up."

"I never knew his real name. Everybody called him Snow 'cause he was an albino or somethin'. His skin was so white you could see the veins. Lord, have mercy, he looked a mess the last time I saw him a few years back. He was a straight-up junkie. Didn't even remember me. But the nigger got what he deserved. Low life mother-fucker."

I took my corporate credit card from my wallet. If the waitress didn't appear in the next ten seconds I would just leave the card with the manager. Pick it back up on my way out of the Narcisco-Musikiwa function.

"Your daddy was off somewhere that day. It's a wonder he didn't have you with him, but he didn't."

Lottie had a faraway look in her eyes. I could tell she was reliving that day. Whatever happened I didn't want to know. If it involved me I didn't want to know. If just mentioning it was enough for my mother to sever her relationship with the woman who was more like a sister to her than a cousin, I was better off not knowing about it. My mother was right. Let sleeping dogs lie.

"Your momma was a little intimidated by all them big city folk so she'd try to pretend like she was some kind of bad ass bitch instead of a plain ol' country girl. Snow scared me though. I ain't shamed to say it. His eyes was red and beady like a rat. Mother-fucker gave me the creeps." Lottie shuddered and lit another cigarette even though the one she'd been smoking still smoldered in the ash tray. "When the doorbell rang and I seen it was him, I told your momma not to let him in. Just wait 'til Sonny get back but you know she didn't never want nobody telling her what to do."

"Can you find out where the Musikiwa party is?" I asked when the waitress retrieved my credit card.

Lottie stopped talking and stared off in the distance keeping whatever recollection that preoccupied her to herself. Thank God. She shook her head as the waitress brought over a fresh pitcher of orange juice.

"Girl, just leave his sorry ass out there on the door step I keep telling her. But she let him in while she went to get the package he came for. I kept telling her who gives a shit what he wants. Let his ass stand out in the cold all fuckin' day for all I cared, but you're momma was always trying to be nice, you know?"

I nodded in agreement even though I didn't know that side of her.

"You know we was from the country where people's always mannerable-like. You'd never leave nobody standing out in the cold or not offer them something cold to drink on a hot day but," and Lottie emphasized the word *but*, "That was in the country. Things was different up here."

I massaged my temples and hoped the throbbing in my head wouldn't turn into a full-blown migraine.

"So when your momma decided to let him in I told her I was going to the store. I didn't want to be in the same house with that bastard." Lottie looked at me. "I'm sorry, baby. I sure am sorry."

Even as I asked the question I wasn't sure that I wanted to hear the answer. "What happened?"

"I guess while your momma was upstairs making a little package for Snow, you woke up from your nap and came downstairs."

I had never noticed the resemblance between my mother and Lottie before.

"When I was on my way down the street Sonny pulled up so I turned around. He and I walked in the house together."

I wanted Lottie to just say it. Whatever it was, I just wanted her to say it so the story could be finished. So I could say good night and get on with my life, a life that no longer included my mother and a life that had never included my father.

"I'll never forget that mother-fucker's little dick. It was long like a pencil. He was standing over you with his dick in his hand and you was just standing there staring at him. You wasn't crying or nothing so we knew he hadn't done nothing. Was 'bout to, but hadn't done nothing yet."

I breathed a sigh of relief.

"Lord have Mercy, I thought Sonny was going to kill that man. You know your daddy had a reputation for being Mr. Cool. Mr. *Savor Faire*. Well, Lord Jesus, Sonny cursed that man and beat the living shit out him. *That's* when you started screaming." She lit another cigarette. "With all the commotion your momma came running from downstairs." Lottie shook her head."You know what she was thinking? She seed old pencil-dick Snow with his pants down begging your daddy for mercy. I swear to God, I don't know who was screaming more. You were balling at the top of your lungs. Sonny was cursing like a mad man. Snow was begging for mercy. Lord Jesus, it was like a scene from hell. When your momma ran down the stairs she grabbed you and hugged you so tight I think that scared you even more. You really went to hollering."

My head was too small to contain the throbbing inside it.

"Sonny yelled for me to open the door and he literally threw Snow out onto the street."

"So nothing happened? Nothing happened to me, right? He didn't molest me, right?"

Lottie patted my hand. "No, baby he didn't molest you. But ..."

"But what?"

"Sonny lit into your momma. Asked her what kind of mother she was. You know you was her soft spot? From the day she found out she was pregnant to the day she died you was her best thing, her light. You know that, don't you?"

I hadn't been completely sure before this moment.

"Sonny asked her, what kind of mother don't know how to keep her own child safe? Then he told her he couldn't stand the sight of her. She was saying something, tell you the truth I don't even remember what it was, but Sonny wasn't having no part of it. She was begging him to listen but he was steady walking for the door."

"He left her? Because of me?"

"I can remember her standing in the doorway, crying and begging Sonny not to go."

My mother? My mother? Was she really talking about my mother?

"But when he got in that Cadillac and drove off he took something that your mother was never able to get back."

Lottie looked at her watch. "Oh shit, girl, let me get my ass out of here. The number twelve don't run but every hour so I don't want to miss it." Lottie scribbled a phone number on a napkin. "This is Keasha's number. That's where I'm staying at. She my baby and the only one of my no account chil'ren that amounted to a hill of beans."

I took the piece of paper and stuffed it in my purse. I scribbled mine down and pressed it along with a fifty dollar bill into my cousin's hand.

"Take a taxi. It's late."

"Girl, I been taking the bus all my life."

"For me?" My lower lip quivered. "Take a taxi for me, okay? I don't want to worry about you being out there all by yourself."

She nodded. "Thank you, baby. Your momma was always bragging 'bout how you making that long dollar. Good for you girl. I always knew you was special. Thank you Lord Jesus for your blessings. Let's stay in touch, all right? I want you to come and see my grandbabies."

I promised that I would. We stood and I wrapped my arms around her and held on until my head stopped spinning. As we walked to the revolving doors at the front of the lobby, she said, "Lord Jesus we didn't even get to talk about you. You got any children?"

I shook my head.

"Don't let all that pretty hair go to waste. You want to pass that shit on, have a pretty little girl that'll look just like you. Shame your momma won't get to see her. My grandbabies are bad as hell but I love 'em to death."

"I'll call you over the weekend. We can catch up then, okay?"

"You be sure to. Don't just say it."

I watched my cousin disappear into a waiting taxi. Fifteen minutes, I told myself. I'll go to this party, put in an appearance, stay for fifteen minutes then take my ass home. It had been a long day.

## Chapter 29 – Maya

A huge banner emblazoned with the combined Narcisco and Musikiwa logos took up almost the entire expanse of the back wall of the hotel ballroom. The celebration that had been going on since lunch time was winding to an end. Only a few stragglers remained. The wait staff circled like vultures removing the carcasses of half eaten appetizers and discarded beverage glasses. I was relieved I'd only have to feign happiness for a few well-wishers who appeared to be too inebriated to notice the mood I was in.

"My God, what a party." Maggie stumbled over to me.

She was more than a little buzzed but she deserved to let loose. Pulling together an event like this with only a few hours notice was a monumental feat. I resisted the urge to remove the champagne glass from her hand. Maybe my maternal instincts were stronger than I gave myself credit for.

"I had started to worry you weren't coming." She lowered her voice and leaned into me as though we were girlfriends sharing a *tête-à-tête*. "You know how evil Mr. Caplin can get when he doesn't get his way."

I didn't comment.

"But here you are." She laughed as if she were watching *Def Comedy Jam*. "He told me to tell you to meet him in his suite after the party to finish the business you started this morning."

I told her I would and watched as she toddled away. Once again, I checked the display screen of my mobile phone. Still no messages. I took a deep breath, squared my shoulders and headed toward the elevator.

I knocked lightly on the door of James' suite. He didn't stand when I entered the most beautifully appointed room I'd ever seen. Smooth jazz played from invisible speakers. The lights were so low I blinked several times to adjust to the dimness in which the room was bathed.

"Would you like champagne?" He held up a bottle of Kristal. He and Lillian operated from the same playbook.

"No thank you."

He sat on the edge of a king sized bed wearing a silk robe. His feet were bare and it seemed he had recently had a pedicure. He patted the space beside him. "Come here."

I made a perfunctory step toward him. "I'm really tired. It's been a long day. Can't we finish whatever needs to be done in the morning?"

He got up and walked over to me. "If Mohammed won't come to the mountain, the mountain will come to Mohammed."

It took all my willpower not to step back but I forced myself to not break eye contact with him. Predators attack when you show fear. I'd watched enough animal kingdom shows to know that. "Mr. Caplin, please."

"I told you to call me James."

He handed me a flute of champagne. This time I accepted it and consumed the contents in a couple of sips. I immediately regretted my decision. I felt light headed.

"That's more like it." He smiled and circled me like a lion sizing up an antelope. His breath was warm against the back of my neck. My entire body tensed when he touched my shoulders and began to gently but firmly massage them. I would never acknowledge it but his touch actually felt good.

"Relax. This night is for celebration." He lifted my hair and kissed the back of my neck.

The soft haze that had temporarily invaded my brain evaporated. I stepped away from him. "Mr. Caplin, James, please, don't do this." I looked straight into his eyes. I was almost as tall as he was. "Let's just forget any of this happened, okay?"

He shook his head. "No, let's pretend we're in Vegas. What happens in this room, stays in this room." He winked at me.

"I'm calling it a night."

He grabbed my arm to prevent me from leaving. "Everyone is really excited about the news." When I turned back to face him he let my arm go and sipped his champagne.

"Is there something you want me to prepare for the morning?"

He brushed his hand across my breasts. "But no one is half as excited as I am right now."

"Get your fuckin' hands off me," I hissed. Enough was enough.

He dropped his hands to his side and set down his champagne flute. We stared at one another as though we were boxers sizing each other up in preparation for the title fight.

"Acquisition time can be a really tricky period in a

*Surrender to Love*

company's history."

As if I had stepped too close to a live electric wire, all my senses tingled. He filled his glass and gestured toward my empty one. I shook my head.

"Have you ever been a part of an organization that was purchased?"

"No."

"No one is surprised by anything that happens. Whether it's when people get promoted," he interrupted himself to sip his drink, "Or people are let go."

"Are you threatening me?"

"You have a lot at stake, Maya." He never lowered his gaze. "The stock you were just issued is restricted for the next twenty-four months. You can't do anything with it unless you stick around."

I broke eye contact. I hadn't realized that.

He untied his bathrobe. The silk garment fell into a puddle on the floor at his bare feet. "For a white guy I've been told I'm pretty well hung."

I gasped at the sight of his pink penis. "Someone's been lying to you." I walked out of the room and slammed the door as hard as I could.

# Chapter 30 – Maya

I turned out of the hotel's underground parking garage and pulled into traffic. Not until I found myself headed south on Lake Shore Drive did I realize the destination to which I was headed. When I pulled into the gates of Oak Wood Cemetery, the most significant historic cemetery on Chicago's south side, the final resting spot of Olympian Jesse Owens, civil rights activist, Ida B. Wells, Chicago Mayor Harold Washington and my mother, Sissy Louise Latimer,

I felt as though my heart was breaking. I knelt down and brushed the debris from my mother's headstone. When it was clear, I stood and stared off in silence. I felt the presence of the people who lay beneath my feet, rich and poor, male and female, all had come to the

*Surrender to Love*

same end, a coffin buried beneath eight feet of dirt.

"Momma?" I waited several seconds as if I expected her to answer. "Why didn't you let me know you?" Dried leaves blew in the wind. "Did you think I wouldn't love you?" Hot tears rolled down my cheeks. I wiped my nose on the sleeve of my jacket. "Maybe I could have even liked you." I looked around the darkened cemetery prepared to be swallowed by the chasm that might open in the universe at my revelation. I had loved my mother but I didn't always like her. If we hadn't been related, I doubt that I would have chosen to pursue a friendship with her. I'd never allowed myself to openly acknowledge that truth before.

What was it momma? Was it fear that kept you from sharing yourself with me? From allowing me to get to know you? Fear that your way of loving was too deep? That if you allowed yourself to give in to it, like Alice, you would fall down a looking glass into a land where things no longer made sense? Silence, interrupted by an occasional bit of traffic noise, was the only reply.

"Did you still love him, momma?" I asked the tombstone at my feet. "When you died, did you still long for my father's touch?" I used to think that, forever, I would feel that way about Deuce but one day I realized days had passed and I hadn't thought of him; then weeks went by and now only on occasion I thought about him. In time, I'm sure I won't think of him at all. Did it never become that way for you, momma? Could you never shake off your feelings for my father?

I ran my hand along the smoothness of the marble headstone. "I wished I had known about you and Sonny," I whispered. I could have empathized with you. We could have shared our feelings and supported one another's strategies for distancing ourselves from the men and emotions that were not good for us. I understood the folly and foolishness of a woman's heart. Even after Deuce showed me that he didn't love me, even after he suggested I give our child to a woman he professed to have never loved, I still loved him. When he called the night before I was to have the procedure, after he desecrated my home by bringing that woman, his wife, into it, because *I* loved him, I was foolish enough to believe *he* loved me. I thought that I had been too quick to judge him, so when Deuce asked to come over, at first I was strong and told him, "Why the fuck would I want that?"

But when he said, "Because I love you. And I'm sorry. And I'll die if you don't forgive me," I immediately weakened.

Momma, were you like me about Deuce when it came to my father? Defenseless? Unable to protect yourself from yourself? Though I knew I shouldn't have given in, I heard myself say, "All right. Be here in twenty minutes." When the dial tone sounded on the other end of the line I raced like a crazy woman to the shower. I rubbed a loofah mitt over my legs and thighs, paid special attention to the heels of my feet. Deuce told me I had the softest skin he'd ever felt. I didn't want to disappoint him, not that I planned to let him touch me, I told myself. I toweled off and smoothed a rich emollient over my skin.

"Chocolate silk. Baby, you feel like chocolate silk." That's what Deuce used to say to me. What was the line my father used on you, momma, that caused you to get wet everytime he uttered it?

That night while I prepared for Deuce, I observed my naked body in the full-length mirror. Only six weeks pregnant but already my breasts had started to swell. Or at least I imagined they had. I laid my hand over my stomach and tried to envision what I would have looked like when it was swollen and taunt. Would I keep my pubic hair thick and bushy the way Deuce liked it if I'd made a different decision? If he had wanted to raise our child with me?

I applied Starry Night Blue liner around my thickly lashed eyes, added just a touch of Satin Rose gloss to my lips. I didn't want to look too made up. I pulled a pale pink satin chemise around my waist and sunk into the pillows of my leather sofa. It was two hours before the doorbell rang.

"Hey baby, sorry I'm late." He stumbled into my condo. "I got tied up." He poured himself a shot of scotch, Chivas Regal, his favorite brand that I kept stocked for his pleasure. "Want something?" He cut his eyes toward me. I didn't respond. He didn't repeat the question.

Did my father treat you that way? After you had slaved in a hot kitchen making his favorite meals, did you watch the grease congeal over the food you'd prepared as it grew cold while you waited? How many times did your world-famous macaroni and cheese casserole dry out because it stayed too long in the oven while you tried to keep it warm for him?

"You said you were coming straight over," I said to Deuce when he finally showed up.

"Fuck." Deuce turned around so quickly he spilled half his drink. "I'm here now, ain't I?" When he was angry, he had a tendency to forget the lessons taught to him by the diction coach he'd hired early on in his career. "Am I supposed to be at your beck-and-call every fucking minute of the day?" He stood in front of me, his face so close to mine I was able to smell more than just liquor on his breath. "I didn't have to come at all. You know that?" He inched closer to me and pointed his finger at my face."You know that don't you?"

I stepped back and turned away from him. I looked down at my bare feet and waited for the anger to come. I waited for it to simmer, then come to a full rolling boil so that I could tell him to get out of my house, to get out of my life, forever. "I'm such a fool," I said barely above a whisper. Is that how you felt about yourself, momma? Did you feel that way, too?

Deuce fell onto the couch. "Oh, no, let me freshen my drink. I feel another one of those psycho-bullshit-you're-not-the-man-I-thought-you-were talks coming on."

I blinked back unshed tears. I shook my head. "No, we're not going to have another one of those conversations." It wasn't him. It was me.

He set down his drink and walked toward me. I stepped back. "I'm such an imposter. Everybody thinks I've really got my act together when in reality what do I have?"

"You've got me."

There was no humor in my laugh. "Like hell, I do."

Because I possessed no will when it came to him, I let Deuce lead me to the sofa and pull me gently down. Like a child in prayer, he knelt before me, laying his head in my lap.

"I'm sorry I hurt you, Maya-girl. You know I love you more than anybody ever loved anything."

I shook my head in the darkness.

"I was just upset. You know I'll do the right thing."

"I don't know anything."

He looked up at me. "Please don't be mad at me."

As if my hand had a will of its own, I stroked his hair.

"It's just that when you told me you were pregnant it reminded me of Sandy. I married her because she was pregnant. And I regretted that decision every day of my life. I tried to do the right thing by her and see where it's gotten me?"

He eased his body up on to the couch.

"After all our time together, don't you know, I'm not Sandy?"

"The last thing I want to talk about is that bitch." Deuce extended his hand to me. "Come on." I followed him into my bedroom. "Lie down. Let me take care of you. You want tea or something?"

"No, thank you."

"What do you want?"

"For you to tell me everything is going to be all right."

He slipped beneath the covers next to me and stroked my flesh. "Don't worry. Everything is going to be all right." He released my breasts from my night gown and suckled them as if he were the baby I wasn't going to have.

"And tell me that you love me." I pushed my body closer to him.

"I love you. You know that." He pulled the gown over my head.

"And tell me that you are never going to leave me." I whimpered as his fingers played inside my wetness.

"Why would I leave the most wonderful woman in the world?"

"Are you still going to love me when my belly is sticking out to here?" I held my hand about a foot above my stomach.

"I thought you made an appointment."

I raised myself up and looked at him. "I did but I'll cancel it."

He chuckled. "Sandy would roast my balls for lunch if she found out you had the baby. That Jew-brother of hers would have my ass in court so fast she'd get all my money and half my dreams." He chuckled again.

"You wouldn't have to say anything to her about the baby until the divorce was final."

He sat up on the side of the bed. "Divorce?"

"You said everything was going to be okay."

"It will, but we have to be patient. If I brought up divorce now she'd take me to the cleaners."

"What about the baby?"

"I was able to clear my calendar for the entire morning. I can go with you. Afterwards we could go to lunch. There's a new Italian place I want to check out."

I saw his lips moving but couldn't understand the words that came out. The blaring of the sirens in my head had become too loud.

"Momma, I'm so sorry my father broke your heart. I know what it feels like."

I tried to remember the last time I heard my mother laugh. Really laugh. Laughed the way my best friends and I sometimes laughed. Laughed until tears rolled down our cheeks and we'd accidentally wet our panties. I couldn't remember. I'm not sure that it ever happened. Growing up, our home wasn't filled with laughter. Occasionally, Lottie and a member or two of her brood would stop by, mostly because they wanted something, usually money. Once in a while a member of the church would come over if there was a specific purpose for the visit, delivery of a choir robe or collection of dues. But after we moved to the house we never joined another church, so even those visits ground to a halt.

My mother had no girlfriends who lounged around our kitchen table sipping coffee and sharing gossip. No gentlemen caller stopped by to take us for a drive on a hot summer's day or stay for Sunday supper.

For the first time, I wondered how long my mother had gone without the feel of a man's skin next to hers or something hard and throbbing inside of her. Since the day my father walked out? Not since I was a little girl?

No wonder her smile was so tight. No wonder laughter never fell through her lips or danced in her eyes. No wonder it had been impossible for me to know the meaning of the smirk that sometimes turned up the corners of my mother's mouth. A Mona Lisa smile; isn't that what it's called? Sissy Louise Latimer, a sixty-year old colored woman from Jericho, Alabama who had come to Chicago, fell in love, had a baby girl and lived the rest of her life with a broken heart.

# Chapter 31 – Maya

When I got home from the cemetery, I put on a pair of flannel pajamas and plopped into bed. Tony's undershirt was still lying on the bedroom floor. It seemed surreal that only this morning I had lain with his flesh inside me. I picked up the undershirt and hugged it to my chest. It smelled of his cologne.

I sighed. There was no way I was going to fall asleep. I reached over and dialed Lillian. That woman is amazing, I thought, when the line was answered on the first ring. Besides me, she was the only person I knew who stayed up late and still got up early.

"Hello?"

I was caught off guard by a man's voice. "Rick?"

"Hell yes, it's Rick. Who else would you expect it to be?"

"Rick, I'm sorry, I didn't mean to disturb you."

"Maya?" His voice softened. "Everything all right?"

"Everything's fine. Tell Lillian I'll give her a call later."

He didn't protest. Before I replaced the receiver the dial tone sounded. I inhaled deeply. "Ohm." I wondered what Tony was doing. "Ohm." I wondered if Cousin Lottie knew where my father was. "Ohm." Did he still live in Chicago? "Ohm." When was the last time my mother had seen him? Stop it, I told myself as I cradled Tony's undershirt in my arms and rocked back and forth. I promised myself I won't to cry, even as tears made wet spots on the linen.

# Chapter 32 – Maya

I watched as a UPS truck rolled to a stop in front of the building. When a tall blonde driver hopped out, I waited for him at the elevator. "Where's Tony?" Even I heard the desperation in my voice. How many other women would ask him that question today? How many of them had Tony made love to? Was it naïve for me to believe I had been the only one?

"Taking a few days off. His sister had a baby so he's helping out or something."

"But I thought she wasn't due until next month?"

The UPS driver shrugged. "Don't know the details, ma'am."

I hoped Brenda and the baby were okay.

# Chapter 33 – Maya

I attempted to log onto my computer without success. *Password is not valid* flashed across the screen. "What the hell?" I mumbled.

"May I come in?"

I looked up and motioned for Carol Henderson, Senior Director of Human Resources at our regional facility, my former boss to enter. Why was she here? When my current boss, James Caplin, followed behind her, I wondered what Herculean task they were about to ask me to perform.

As soon as they were seated Carol said, "Look Maya, you know I'm not one to pussyfoot around so let me just spell it out for you."

Though Carol was speaking, I focused my attention on James.

"With the Musikiwa takeover there are quite a few

redundant positions. I don't have to tell you that," Carol curled her lips into what was supposed to be a smile. "You did most of the analysis."

"Yes?"

"If you know anything about Musikiwa, it's that they run a highly profitable organization. To say that it's lean is an understatement."

As realization of what was about to happen set in, I began shaking my head. "I can't believe this." I stared at James Caplin. I wanted to bitch-slap him.

"Unfortunately, your position is slated for elimination."

The room went black for a split second. I held onto the front of my desk to steady myself.

"We're prepared, of course, to offer you a generous severance package."

I glared at James, "You asshole."

"I understand this must be a shock," Carol said.

I ignored her and continued to speak to him. "You really think you can sweep me aside like yesterday's trash?"

"I'm sorry that you feel that way," she began again.

"Shut up," I yelled at her.

"I'll excuse that because you're upset. I understand that." Her face had taken on a soft pinkish glow.

"Upset? You haven't seen upset."

Carol stood and opened my door. Two security guards stood outside. She beckoned for them to enter. "Security will see you out. We'll send your personal belongings home by courier."

I jerked away from the youngest of the security guards who had taken me by the elbow. "Get your hands off me."

Carol shrugged and the security guard acquiesced and released my arm. As I strode toward the bank of elevators, I ignored the crowd that had gathered, but their eyes felt like daggers in my back.

## Chapter 34 — Maya

As I stumbled onto the sidewalk, I felt blinded by the brightness of the sun. I rummaged in my handbag for a pair of sunglasses but the effort proved greater than I could accomplish. Squinting against the morning glare, I bowed my head and allowed myself to be carried along by the rush hour crowd.

"Waiting for an invitation?" the man behind me growled when I didn't immediately step off the sidewalk into the street when the traffic light turned green. When I turned to look at him, he glared at me as if I were a turd left on the street by an inconsiderate dog owner.

"Sorry," I mumbled as I stepped out of his way. I looked at the street signs and couldn't believe I had walked twenty blocks from the building where I used to work. Could that be true? Could Narcisco Industries, now Musikiwa International, be my former employer? A twelve year successful career down the drain like spilled soda?

"*You* may not, but some of us got places to go," said the man. He bent his head against the wind that had begun blowing and plowed across the street. I watched his progress as he moved with a sense of purpose, as though he owned the sidewalk. Earlier this morning that had been me. Now, I was already thinking of myself in the past tense. Could that be true? In the time that it had taken me to walk from the Narcisco facilities to the corner of State and Roosevelt, had I been transformed from mover-and-shaker to loser? Apparently so. And people who were still upwardly mobile could sense that I was an interloper. I no longer belonged to their club. I felt light-headed.

"You okay?"

It took several seconds before I realized the woman in the jogging suit next to me was talking to me.

"You all right?" she asked again.

It seemed as if her voice were traveling from a great distance before it reached my ears.

"You need me to call somebody for you?" She held up her mobile phone as though she weren't sure I would understand the meaning of her question without the assistance of a visual aid.

I shook my head and smiled. "Yes," I said quickly. "No," I corrected myself. "Thanks, I don't need you to call anyone. I'm fine," I assured her.

She nodded and ran across the street but I saw her look back as if she didn't believe what I said was really true. She was probably right. I spotted a Starbucks at the end of the block and made my way toward it.

"Grande, house blend," I said to the young man working behind the counter.

Without speaking, he nodded and prepared my coffee.

"You like your job?" I asked him when he handed it to me.

At first I didn't think he was going to respond but finally he said, "Yeah, it's cool." Perhaps he had never asked himself that question and he needed time to ponder. "Want me to get you an application?" he asked. "We're hiring."

I thanked him but declined the offer.

"It may seem kind of complicated, but it doesn't take long to get it." He smiled encouragingly. "You could do it."

I took my cup and settled into a corner in the front of the store. "Ohm, ohm, ohm," I chanted silently. Maybe I was dreaming. Maybe none of this was actually happening. "Ohm, ohm, ohm," I chanted as I looked through the plate glass window, the morning rush hour crowd replaced by moms, or perhaps nannies, pushing babies in strollers that cost a small fortune.

"Excuse," said the young man who had served me my drink earlier.

"Yes?"

"Sorry, but we have a two hour limit." He shrugged.

I looked confused.

"I know you're not homeless or anything but rules are rules ..."

I looked at my watch. Four hours had passed. "I'm sorry." I picked up my coffee cup. Its contents were ice cold. "I'm sorry," I said again. I felt tears well in my eyes. "I'm so sorry."

"Don't sweat it," he said. He looked toward the counter where a heavy-set man with pale skin, blood red hair and a tattoo that covered the entire side of his neck was making exotic caffeine-based drinks. "My boss is kind of a stickler for the rules. I don't care, but."

"It's okay," I said again as I walked out into the street and hailed a taxi.

"Good morning, Miss Latimer," said my doorman when I walked into my building. "Is everything all right?"

I shook my head. I didn't trust myself to speak.

"Can I get you anything?" The look of concern on his face seemed genuine. "Should I call somebody?'

I shook my head again. When I walked into my condo I glanced at the telephone. I wasn't sure if I was pleased or disappointed that the call waiting light wasn't flashing. I glanced at the clock. It was after noon, only by a few minutes, but after noon, never-the-less. I poured myself a drink. I thought about calling my girls but wasn't in the mood to talk. I drank my first glass, an Australian Chardonnay. I already felt light-headed. I hadn't eaten anything all day. I poured myself another glass. This time I sipped it. The telephone seemed to beckon me.

"Yes?"

I looked at the receiver, somewhat surprised it was in my hand. "Is that any way to answer the phone?" I asked the familiar voice on the other end of the line. I could hear my words slurring together. I hoped that he couldn't.

He chuckled. "Well, God does answer prayer."

I stopped talking. The way I felt was probably the way an alcoholic who after months of sobriety has taken a drink feels, foolish and disappointed in one's self. Why had I called him? When Deuce and I were together he never supported me, at least not in the way I needed support. There was no reason to believe that had changed.

"Can I see you?" he asked me.

I should just hang up, I told myself. It didn't matter that I was the one who called him. I didn't owe him anything.

"Baby, what's wrong?"

I felt my chin quivering. I felt so lonely. There was no one in my life to call me baby.

"Talk to me. What's the matter?
"I got fired."
"I'll be there in thirty minutes."

The dial tone sounded in my ear. I opened another bottle of wine and poured myself a drink. If an empty bottle of Coldstream Hills Reserve wasn't sitting on the dresser in front of me I would have sworn I hadn't consumed an entire bottle already.

I jumped when the security buzzer sounded. It had only been twenty-three minutes. I wondered what excuse he'd give Sandy for not coming straight home if I let him stay the night; that he was comforting a sick friend? The buzzer sounded again. Two more minutes passed. Would he tell his wife he was on a mission of mercy, like when my mother and I went to rescue Cousin Lottie? The buzzer sounded again followed by the ringing of my home phone. Deuce's voice sounded over the answering machine.

"Maya, it's me. I'm here. Baby, pick up. Do you have any idea how much I've missed you? How much I love you?" he asked me.

I wasn't going to debate him on whether or not his love for me had been real. I chose to believe that he *had* loved me; perhaps he loved me still. But he didn't love me in the way I needed and deserved to me loved. I lifted the receiver and said, "Go home to your wife, Deuce."

"You called me," he said.

"I made a mistake." I hung up the phone. I knew he was pissed. I didn't care.

# Chapter 35 – Maya

I woke up with a splitting headache as the sun streamed through my window. Usually, I was glad that I had won the argument with my interior decorator and not put up a window treatment. The unobstructed view of Lake Michigan offset the slightly off-balanced look of the room but this morning I wished I had black-out drapes so that I could pull them to block the sun.

My mouth felt like a field of cotton had been planted in it. I should get up, I told myself. Take a shower, get dressed. But I didn't have anywhere to go. There was no one I wanted to see. Well, there *was* one person but he no longer wanted to see me. I smoothed the wrinkles from Tony's undershirt. It still smelled of his cologne. I cradled it beneath my cheek. When I woke up again, another day had passed.

# Chapter 36 — Maya

I dragged myself from bed and shuffled into the living room. My hair was matted to the back of my head. My mouth felt like moss was growing on my teeth. The message waiting light blinked on my phone. I scanned through the phone numbers that had been stored in the caller ID. None of them belonged to Tony. My mother was right. I was going to be a fool forever. I doubted that I was the first woman for whom Tony had made a play. As fine as he was he was probably screwing a different woman on every floor of the building. Even as I said that, I knew it wasn't true. Tony and I had made a connection. It was real. I knew in my heart that it was real.

After washing my face and brushing my teeth, I felt better. I raked a comb through my hair and parted it down the middle, braiding it into two long plaits like my mother used to do when I was a child. I poured myself a large glass of orange juice. The sugar hit my system like a shot of adrenaline to the heart. "I really messed up this time, didn't I, mommy?"

My longing for her felt like a physical weight pressing against my chest. I rummaged around my apartment and collected all the old photographs I could find. "There's a project for you," I said out loud then chuckled. "Note to self," I said out loud, "Stop talking to yourself about yourself, especially in the third person."

I sat on the floor and spread the pictures all around me. Images of me and my mother, from my birth to her death, stared up at me. I picked up a photograph and smiled. I remembered when this one was taken. I stood in front of her, her arms resting on my shoulders. We were both looking directly into the camera grinning like Cheshire cats. She had on her maroon choir robe. That had been my favorite. That was the one she wore when she performed with the Women's Gospel Choir and they sang contemporary gospel songs authored by people like Fred Hammond or CeCe Winans, and not the traditional hymnals written by old white men who lived a hundred years ago.

It wasn't often my mother and I went back to evening services since we attended both morning services but the pastor, Reverend Grayson, had made a special request that she sing that evening. The church was having a mortgage celebration party. One of the deacons, Mr. Hershey, came to pick us up and committed to bring us back home. "What kind of celebration it's going to be, Sister Latimer, if you ain't there to raise your voice in song?" the pastor had asked her. When we walked in the church we were greeted like visiting luminaries. I was scooped away to play with the other kids while my mother changed into her robe.

"'Bout time for you to get baptized, ain't it?" the pastor asked me. I looked to my mother for guidance but she had already entered the back room. Before I was forced to answer, Reverend Grayson's attention was pulled to elsewhere and he moved on.

I looked through the stack of pictures and found three more of my mother and me from that day. It wasn't long after they had been taken that we moved to the house. And the way the buses ran, we would have to get up too early and stay too long after service had ended to continue our membership at New Salem. I hadn't been there since I was a child. I wondered if it was still on the corner of Cleveland Avenue and Morning Glory lane.

In less than thirty minutes, I was in the car driving toward my old neighborhood. Until I went with Tony to the skating rink, I hadn't been on the south side since I graduated from high school. When I went away to college and my mother moved downtown, I had no reason to travel past downtown.

I pulled to a stop in front of my old church. If the sign out front didn't read New Salem Missionary Baptist Church, I would not have believed it to be the same place. It seemed so much smaller than I remembered, and so much more run-down. Like a cobra hypnotized by the playing of a snake charmer, I felt drawn to the music coming from inside as I walked up the stairs and entered the lobby that still felt familiar. How many times had I stood there waiting for my mother to change clothes and retrieve me for our solitary bus ride home?

"Excuse me, miss."

I turned around. It was Pastor Grayson, older and more feeble, but I knew it was him. I wondered if he still had the stamina to race around the church like he did twenty years ago when my mother would sing. "Pastor Grayson?"

*Surrender to Love*

He walked toward me. "You here for bible study?"

I planned to tell him that I had only come to visit for old time sake, but he hooked his arm through mine and continued, "It's down this way. We's meeting in the small Sunday School room today. Choir's practicing for the special meeting this Sunday. You coming, ain't you? Remembrance Sunday, that's what we calling it."

His eyes were cloudy with phlegm. Hearing aids were wedged in both his ears. "A time to remember and give thanks for all those peoples we loved who have died and gone on to glory."

"I'm going to try," I said. It felt good to be here. I hadn't been inside a church since Lillian's wedding. It felt peaceful here. I could tell Pastor Grayson needed my support as we shuffled down the hall. I assumed he was too vain to use a cane even though he had to be at least in his mid-eighties, maybe older. The limited amount of gray hair could be compliments of a tube not youthfulness. A contemporary Kirk Franklin song spilled from the sanctuary.

"My mother used to sing in the choir," I said.

He stopped. I wasn't sure if it was because he wanted to get a closer look at me or if he needed to rest. "Who your momma is?" he asked.

"Sissy Latimer."

He looked as if he were trying to see through me. "Lawd, have mercy." He released his grip on my elbow and walked a few paces ahead of me then turned around and looked at me again. "Sister Latimer, where in the heck have you been? Why ain't you been to service?" He shook his head and smiled as though he couldn't believe his good fortune. "Can you sing this Sunday?"

"I'm not Sissy. Sissy Latimer was my mother."

He lowered his voice and whispered to me, "Girl, we ain't had no good singing since you left." This time when he took my arm he was leading, not leaning on me. When he pushed through the doors of the sanctuary, he called out, "Look who's here."

The members of the thirty person choir stopped singing and stared at us.

"Sissy Latimer. She done come back." With me in tow, he shuffled down the aisle toward the pulpit. I assumed he was speaking to the woman directing the choir. She looked vaguely familiar. "I know you going to say you got the program all set but you got to make a place for this lady. She one of the mothers of the church. Been with us since you was a little bitty girl." That's where I'd seen her. She used to sing in the youth choir when my mother and I regularly attended service here.

I shook my head and started to protest.

"All right, Reverend Grayson," the woman said, "Whatever you want we'll try to accommodate."

A young man stepped out of formation and walked down the stairs. "Grandpa, want me take you to bible study? Shouldn't you be in bible study right now? You're going to be late. And you know you don't like it when they start without you."

"I *was* on my way to bible study." Reverend Grayson looked around as though he wasn't sure how he had ended up in the sanctuary.

"I don't sing," I began. The choir director shook her head in understanding. "He's a little forgetful," she whispered. "Alzheimer's."

"I can take him to bible study," I volunteered. "No need to interrupt your rehearsal."

"You sure?" asked the young man.

"C'mon, Reverend Grayson," I said. "You were going to show me where the class was meeting today."

Reverend Grayson looked at me as though he were seeing me for the first time. "Well, I may be old but I ain't so old I don't appreciate the company of a pretty lady."

I chuckled.

"You better watch him," the young man said.

*Surrender to Love*

"Grandpa's a smooth talker."

"I'll be careful," I promised as we resumed our journey.

A short, heavy set woman spoke to a group of eight people. "There you are," she said when I entered the room with Reverend Grayson. "We were wondering where you were."

"Sorry," I volunteered. "I distracted him."

"Now who you say you is?" he asked me.

"We'll talk after class," I promised.

The small group turned back to their female leader. She wore a name tag with Ethel printed in bold, black letters. A woman with soft brown eyes laid a bible opened to the text they were studying in front of me.

"How we answer the questions about what happens to us in the life after death can have profound implications for how we understand our lives here and now," she said.

"Amen," said the woman with the soft brown eyes.

"It can set the context for how we face the ups and downs that are an inevitable part of life."

Several of the people nodded.

"During slavery times, the masters thought teaching Christianity would keep their slaves docile, but the slaves heard another meaning. They identified with the people of Israel, people who were once slaves in Egypt. Stories of their escape through the Red Sea let our ancestors know it was possible for miracles to occur, like a Harriet Tubman appearing out of nowhere to lead them through the perils of the night to freedom on the Underground Railroad."

"Yes, Jesus."

"We from a mighty people," said Reverend Grayson.

"Thank you, Lord."

"Praise you, Jesus."

I thought about Cousin Lottie.

"Jesus," said the bible study leader, "Jesus, is the

face of God turned toward the world." The woman sounded as if she were about to preach not just teach. "And Jesus is the face of love turned toward us if we choose to see."

I checked my watch even though I knew I had nowhere to go.

"No matter what we've achieved or failed to achieve; no matter how many degrees we've earned or at what grade we dropped out of school; no matter how many times we got it right or how many tries we've screwed things up, the meaning of Jesus' life and death and resurrection is that God won't forsake us. He'll never leave us alone."

I fidgeted with the bible laying open in front of me.

"Ladies and gentlemen, can you read with me from your bibles? Romans, chapter eight, verses thirty-eight through thirty-nine?"

I watched as everyone picked up their bibles. I did, too, and I read out loud with the class, "For I am convinced that neither death, nor life, nor angels, nor rulers, nor things present, nor things to come, nor powers nor height, nor depth, nor anything else in all creation, will be able to separate us from the love of God in Christ Jesus, our Lord." As I closed my bible, I felt my spirit soar.

# Chapter 37 – Maya

I sat at a table in the back of swanky restaurant and watched the beautiful people strolling up and down Michigan Avenue. I had probably lost six pounds over my self-imposed exile. I couldn't remember the last time I'd eaten anything. But I felt good again. Better than good, liberated even.

I stood and waved as Donna entered the restaurant. She hugged me tightly before we sat down to order. "Are you all right?" she demanded. "I've been worried sick about you. There are some pretty crazy rumors flying around work about you. You haven't answered your phone for the past three days. And that maximum security building you live in won't tell nobody nothing."

I waved my hand in dismissal. "I'm fine. Honest."

*Surrender to Love*

"Then I need to kick your ass." She was seriously pissed with me. "You need to call Lillian, too. That girl's about to hire storm troopers to break into your place."

"Sorry, girlfriend. Forgive me?" I hadn't thought about how my disappearance would affect my friends.

"You paying for lunch?"

"Of course." I could tell she was still upset, but she was a strong advocate of respecting people's privacy.

"Okay, I forgive you," she finally said. The waitress handed us menus. "So, what's good here? I'm starving. As usual." I guessed she added that before I said anything. Even I was getting concerned about the amount of weight she had gained. Comforting oneself was one thing; high blood pressure and diabetes were another.

"Donna, I'm finally doing it," I said as soon as she closed her menu.

"You're kidding? No wonder you've been underground." She lowered her voice and whispered to me, "You're getting married? To who? Oh shit, not Deuce? Girlfriend, tell me not to his two-foot tall ass?"

"No," I shouted louder than I had intended. "I'm not getting married."

"Then what the hell are you talking about?"

"Starting the business we used to talk about."

"Oh that." She picked up her menu and perused the lunch specials again.

"I pulled out the business plan I did for my MBA, so it's from about five years ago. It needs a little updating, but the mission, the vision, the marketing plan are still solid. I'm ready to do it, start my own thing and I can't think of anyone else who I'd rather partner with."

Donna closed her menu and stared at me. "Girlfriend, thanks for thinking of me, but been there, done that."

I shook my head in confusion. "What do you mean?"

"Didn't you know I used to own my own business?"

"No." How could I not know that? I thought we

shared everything. I guess each of us had our secrets.

"I don't talk about it much. Lord knows I'm trying to forget it." Donna waved to the waitress. After we placed our orders she continued, "I opened a grocery store in the hood, three blocks from where I grew up."

"Really?"

"Organically grown greens that were so clean you could just take them from the bag and cook 'em; yams so sweet you didn't need sugar, and you know what?"

"What?" I don't know why I even asked. I already knew how this story would end.

"The community didn't support it." She shrugged but tears gathered in the corners of her eyes. "People complained that the greens were forty cent a pound more than the grocery store chain where not a single black person was in management even though ninety-five percent of the customers and staff were black. They whined because the chickens weren't plump enough." She sighed. "Of course not, mine were free range, not that crap you buy at the grocery store plumped up with growth hormones."

I massaged my temples.

"That little flight of fancy not only left me broke..." She paused and blinked several times before she continued, "I know that's what ended my marriage. Bradley could never understand why I quit a hundred thousand dollar a year job, invested my entire 401(k) in a venture that, at best, would only break even. But it wasn't just about the money, you know?"

"What was it about?"

She grunted."You sound like Bradley. Ain't everything about money, you know?"

I imagined I probably looked like a deer caught in the headlights while I stared at her.

"It was about doing something good, giving something back, but in the end ..." She shrugged. "It became all about the money. Or more accurately our

*Surrender to Love*

lack of it. We couldn't adjust our lifestyle to the new reality of our finances. He never admitted it, but I think he couldn't get over being angry at me for putting us in that position. He kept saying he was too old to start over ... now look at us ... talk about starting over."

The server set our entrees in front of us. "Good luck, girl. I may talk shit but I was happy as a pig in mud when I got the job with Narcisco." Donna set down her fork. "I hoped when I started making money again, me and Bradley could get it back together, but ..." She shrugged again. I hadn't realized she still had such strong feelings for the man.

"Saying sorry don't always make everything okay." She cut into her prime rib sandwich. "Girlfriend, don't let me discourage you though. If anyone can make it work it's you. But me," she poked her finger into her chest. "Me, I'm keeping my ass right at Musikiwa International working for Mr. Charlie because, right now, I ain't got a man or a retirement fund."

# Chapter 38 – Tony

I fully extended my arms. Four days and counting. I hadn't returned Maya's phone calls but my resolve was weakening. If I saw her number on the caller identification one more time I don't think I would have been able to resist picking up.

"You need to check yourself, big brother," Brenda told me when I told her about my last encounter with Maya.

I had to agree.

"The one thing all you're failed relationships have in common is you. That's a clue that you need to rethink *your* game."

I allowed my muscles to feel the full weight of the bar over my upper chest before I lowered it back into the rack. I sat up and wiped the sweat from my face.

"I'm impressed."

I turned and smiled at the woman sitting on the weight bench next to me.

"You're in *great* shape," she said.

Her body was thin but not bony, her muscles well-defined. Her straight black hair was pulled into a loose pony tail.

"For a man my age," I added. Most mornings, I had a nagging pain in my lower back when I first woke up. Getting old was a bitch.

She laughed. "That's not what I'm saying at all." I couldn't tell if she was a hundred percent Asian or mixed race like Russell Simmon's ex-wife Kimora.

"Now you," I said, "Are in great shape." And she was. She wasn't in the kind of shape I liked, but she was in magazine model shape. For my liking she was too athletic, not enough curves, but I was a man who loved black women. Not that black women seemed to love me back. Maybe it was time to try something new. That's what Brenda kept telling me.

"Stop dating the same bitch over and over. Their names change but the profile's the same." Of course Brenda had meant a different type of black woman, not a different race of woman.

The woman extended her hand. "Rebecca," she said. "My friends call me Becca."

"So what should I call you?" I smiled. "I've seen you around the gym but I don't presume we're friends." We relinquished the equipment we'd been using to another couple. "But I'd like to be," I added.

Becca laughed. She had a beautiful smile.

"I'm Tony by the way."

I shook Becca's hand. Her grip was firm, her skin was soft.

"Well Tony-by-the-way, have time to grab a quick bite? We could talk about what it takes to be my friend."

"Give me ten minutes to shower. I'll meet you out front."

The warm water caressed my muscles like a masseuse. I thought about my mother. Not a good sign. "Good looking boy like you got to be careful," she had warned me when I turned sixteen and started working in the shipping and receiving dock of a warehouse on the edge of downtown. "Specially with these low-down white heifers. They'll have sex with you at night then cry rape in the morning. You can't trust 'em. I've been around 'em all my life."

"Come on, mama, I thought that's what the civil rights movement was all about?"

"You think people fought and died to give you a chance to mess around with white girls?"

"You know what I mean. To give me a choice. To expand my rights."

She kneaded dough for the biscuits she was making to go with the pork chops and home fries we were having for dinner. Moms made sure a brother had a full belly when he got up from the table. That's also why she taught me how to cook.

"Of course, you got the right to do it. I'm just hoping you choose not to. That's all I'm saying. When I look at my daughter-in-law, I want to see somebody who looks like me."

It only took a few minutes for me to towel off and get dressed. When I walked into the lobby Becca stood up. "Ready?"

She had changed into a black mini skirt and boots. Her ass was as flat as my stomach. She wasn't wearing a bra under her tank top. Her boobs looked like golf balls with nipples.

"I apologize for keeping you waiting."

"No biggie. Where'd you like to go? There's a little coffee shop around the corner. They make pretty good salads and sandwiches."

"That's the thing, I changed my mind. I'm ..." The sentence trailed off into silence. I wasn't sure how to articulate why I changed my mind.

"Hey, don't explain. It really is no big deal." She slung her duffle bag over her shoulder. "See you around?"

I nodded. Perhaps Wesley Snipes was on to something. I knew a lot of sisters who would have gone off if I'd kept them waiting then blew them off. Asian women might bring a different vibe to the game. But it was too late to teach this old dog new tricks. I was a black man who loved himself some black women.

# Chapter 39 – Maya

Lillian, dressed in a designer sweat suit and sneakers that cost more than most people's dress shoes flung open the front door. "Where the hell have you been?" she demanded as I walked into the house.

"It's a long story." I plopped down on the living room sofa.

Lillian sat across from me. She glared at me for several seconds. I could tell she was trying to cool off before she began talking. "Look, I'm sorry I couldn't talk to you the other night when you called but I know that's not why you haven't returned my calls."

"Of course not," I assured her. I felt like getting an attitude that she would even think something like that.

"Rick surprised me and came home early."

"Good for you, girlfriend." I meant that.

"Who you telling? He put it on me like the old days. If

*Surrender to Love*

my tubes weren't tied we would have made a baby that night." She leaned forward and whispered, "He's been missing me as much as I've been missing him." She shook her head. "I don't care how smart they are, these men can't seem to multi-task." She could tell she'd lost me, so she explained. "He's been working on this really big, complex deal at work. So he had been focused on that instead of this." She pointed to her private parts. "As soon as the deal closed he was back on it."

Though Donna and I teased her about marrying Rick for his money, I knew she really loved him. "Honey, that's great."

When Lillian noticed the smile on my lips didn't reach my eyes, she asked, "What's the matter, girlfriend?"

I opened my mouth to tell her about the incident with my boss but, "Tony and I broke up," popped out of my mouth.

"Who?"

"Tony," I replied, "the UPS man."

"Oh him." She waved her hand in the air as if she were swatting away a fly. "That's no surprise."

"And I got fired from my job." Okay, that's what I had meant to say.

"What?" She got up and hugged me. "What happened? Are you all right?"

That was the reaction I wanted. I needed someone else to be as incensed as I was. I needed someone to share my pain. "My boss basically told me if I didn't fuck him he'd make life difficult for me."

Her eyes widened. "No?"

"So when I told him to go fuck himself, the next day I was informed my services were no longer needed."

She walked around the living room. My girl was pissed. I guess neither of us had lost our southside ghetto roots. I think if I had suggested we go jack his ass, my girl would have been down.

"You can't put nothing past these white folks." She shook her head.

I rummaged through my hand bag and pulled out an audio tape. "But I've got something for his ass."

"Is that what I hope it is?"

I nodded.

"My girl." We gave one another high-fives.

"Clearly, he didn't know who he was dealing with. Southside," we chorused in unison then cracked up laughing.

"I can get you the name of a really good employment attorney from Rick. Remember George Mason?"

I shook my head.

"Yes you do," she insisted. "Used to work with Rick when he was with McKenzie?"

"Oh yeah, tall, good looking brother married to that skinny Swedish blonde who looked like she was on heroin?"

"He divorced her ass. Turned out she *was* on heroin. I knew something was up with that bitch. The woman never ate. I mean never. Chick would go out to dinner with us and order hot water with lemon." I could see Lillian's wheels turning. "I don't think he's remarried, yet."

"Can you stop playing matchmaker for a second?"

"Sorry," she continued, "He sued McKenzie for discrimination and got a half a million dollar settlement. Rick said he let the company off cheap. He could have gotten more."

"Okay, get his name," I said, "But in the meantime I have a proposition for you."

"Don't tempt me. I know Field's is having that big sale but I promised myself I was going to be good and not go."

"I'm not talking about a shopping trip."

"What? The spa?"

"No." I sighed. "How about starting a business with your best friend in the whole wide world?"

She laughed out loud. "Sorry," she apologized. "You

know what, girlfriend? That offer is not even tempting."

"How can you say that? I haven't even told you about it."

"Doesn't matter. There's nothing you could say that would make me want that."

"Come on, Lillian, this is me. I know you love the kids and this whole desperate-housewives-thing but don't you miss work? Even a little?"

"Girlfriend, I *am* working. I'm using every skill I have to manage our home. I have P&L responsibility. I'm a project manager, financial advisor, sales, marketing, public relations, community affairs, you name it, I do it."

I didn't try to hide my disappointment.

"Sorry, girlfriend. Maybe Donna might be interested."

"She already said no."

"You went to *her* before *me*?"

I rolled my eyes. "Don't even start."

"I'm joking." I felt her watching me. "You know, with your credentials another company will snap you up in a second. You're not worried about getting another job, are you?"

I shrugged. "You know what? I'm not really that upset about the job stuff."

"I thought you loved Narcisco?"

"I did love it. It's just that..." I tried to tune in to what I was feeling.

"What?"

I shrugged again. "I don't know," I finally said. I didn't feel like talking about my mother. Or my father. I still hadn't processed all that.

"You okay about breaking up with the UPS man?"

I rolled my eyes at her.

"I mean Tony."

I didn't want to talk about him either. "I don't know."

"What then?"

Tears rolled down my cheeks. Instantly, my girl

wrapped her arms around me. She didn't ask what was wrong. She just held me while I bawled, body-wracking, snot-slinging, ugly-face making sobbing. When I pulled away from her, she handed me a tissue.

"Want to talk about it?"

I thought for a second then shook my head. No. When I realized what I was crying about I felt a burden had been lifted. I was grieving for the embryo that would never grow into a child, for the life that was not meant for me to bring into this world.

"Where are my god sons?" I asked. I longed to see their little faces.

"Sleeping." She snapped her fingers. "Like clock work, I put those little rascals to bed."

"Can I take a peek?"

We tiptoed upstairs. "I can't believe how big they've gotten," I whispered when I looked into their cribs. My heart felt weary that my precious little god sons were growing up in a country that placed lesser value on them because they were of African descent. Maybe things would be different for them.

"I know it sounds cliché but it seems like just yesterday I was telling Rick that I was pregnant. Now look at them. Time is passing so quickly."

I nodded. "Life is short."

I felt tears coming again. "I'm coming over really soon to hang out with my boys, okay?"

"Anytime."

I hugged my girl. "All right, girlfriend, I've got to run. I have a stop to make."

I could tell she wanted to ask me where I was going, but for a change, she kept her mouth shut.

# Chapter 40 – Maya

The Women's Pavilion of St. Joseph's Memorial looked more like an upscale hotel than a hospital. I walked down the hall and knocked softly on a closed door. When I poked my head in, I whispered to the lump that lay in the bed, "Brenda?"

She opened her eyes and smiled. "Maya?" She beckoned for me to come closer to the bed. "Hey girl, long time no see."

I held out a bouquet of flowers. "Congratulations." I sat the flowers on the night stand next to the bed. "I heard you had the baby." Tears instantly sprang into her eyes. I grabbed her hand. "What's the matter?"

When I left her room, I walked down the aisle that led to the neonatal intensive care unit. I stared through the glass windows at four tiny babies, each immersed in his or her own struggle for survival. Since only one

*Surrender to Love*

of them was black, I knew she was Brenda and Dean's little girl.

"What are you doing here?"

I turned around. My heart, literally, seemed to skip a beat at the sight of Tony. He looked taller and thinner since I'd last seen him but that was probably only my imagination. It felt as though it had been a lifetime since I'd laid eyes on him.

"I heard that Brenda had the baby. I just wanted to check in." I turned around and stared through the glass. "She's so tiny."

"But she's a fighter," he said.

I smiled. He would be this little girl's champion. I felt the heat of his body standing behind me. I turned around and faced him. "Look, Tony," I began, "I'm sorry."

He put a finger against my lips to silence me.

"I'm sorry too. It seems like all I do is think about you."

We both laughed.

"See how bad it is? Sounds like I'm quoting song lyrics."

"I've always been a sucker for old school."

"In that case," he said, "I've got some Barry White back at the crib." He wrapped his arms around me and hugged me tightly to his chest. I couldn't believe how good that felt. It was like coming home after a long business trip.

"Make it Teddy Pendergrass and you've got a deal." I looked up into his eyes. He had the longest eyelashes I'd ever seen on a man. He was one fine black brother.

"Oh, before I forget." I opened my purse and took out my checkbook. "Here." I handed him a check made out to Brenda for a thousand dollars. "Can you give this to Brenda? I don't want to wake her up again."

He stared at the check then looked back at me.

"What's this for?"

"She's going to need help with the baby. She can use that to hire a nurse or something."

He held the check for me to take it back. "If she needs help I'll go over there and help her."

"Of course, but you can't be there all the time."

"What about you?"

"What about me?"

"If Brenda needs help, what's wrong with you coming over to help her?"

"Tony, remember, I work for a living?" As soon as I said that I realized that was no longer true. Up until a few days ago it had been. I couldn't imagine it would take that long before it was true again, but now wasn't the time to go into all the work-drama that had transpired since the last time we'd spoken.

"So do I. I work for a living, too."

I took a deep breath. The last thing I wanted was to insult him. I started again. "Look, I understand you're feeling emotional."

"Don't use that tone with me. I'm not one of your employees you're trying to manipulate into believing shutting down their plant and moving operations offshore is a good thing."

I took a deep breath. I didn't want to fight. "I don't understand what you're getting so upset about. I was trying to do a good thing."

He shook his head. "Somebody needs help and your immediate reaction is to open your pocket book?"

"Excuse me for being generous."

"That's my niece, Maya. *I'm* going to be there for her." Tony pounded his chest like Tarzan. "Me. Not a team of hired hands. What's wrong with you women?"

"What women are you referencing?" It was my turn to feel insulted. "Just because I can afford ..." I started the sentence but he didn't let me finish.

He ripped the check in two. "It's not about what you can or can not afford." He rubbed his hand against his chest. "It's about what's in your heart. It's about giving someone your heart." He stepped away from me.

"Maybe you don't care about that baby but I do."

I felt tiny bubbles of anger simmering. "Stop twisting around everything I say," I shouted at him, then lowered my voice when two of the nurses turned around and stared at us. If looks could kill, we would have both fallen dead on the spot. "I do care. You know that I care."

"How would I know that?"

I hesitated, unsure how I should respond. "I'm here. I came here."

"When was the last time you did something for someone? With no expectation of getting something back in return?"

I opened, then closed my mouth. I finally said, "My mother. When she was sick, every day after work I came to the hospital and sat with her."

"I'm sorry about you moms," said Tony. "You know I am."

I nodded.

"But that was your *mother*. And how long ago was that?"

I didn't respond.

"That's what I thought."

"Tony, you're not being fair. When you're working sixty, seventy hours a week, there's not time for anything else."

"That's bullshit, Maya." He lowered his voice. He was talking to me the way he counseled the teenage boys from the North Avenue Project. "People make time for the things that are important to them. For the people who are important to them."

"Mr. Jackson?"

We turned our attention to the doctor who had walked up behind us. "Yes?" he responded.

"It's very serious," said the Neonatologist.

Tony closed then opened his eyes. He mumbled a quick prayer.

"An occlusion," began the doctor.

"Speak English," interrupted Tony.

"An air bubble," I interpreted.

The doctor nodded. "Yes, an air bubble traveled through an open shunt in your niece's brain."

"My God," I said before I caught myself.

"Is she going to be all right?" asked Tony. I stroked his arm.

"She needs an operation."

"Have you told my sister?"

"I thought we'd tell her together."

He nodded. "Thank you, doctor."

Tony and the doctor walked toward Brenda's room. I followed a few paces behind them. Tony stopped and turned to me. "This is family business," he said. "I'll send Brenda your regards."

I watched in silence as they continued their journey without me.

# Chapter 41 – Maya

The red message waiting light on my home phone was flashing when I walked in. It was probably Donna or Lillian, or both of my girls, checking up on me. I loved them but didn't feel like talking to either one of them right now. All I wanted to do was crawl into my bed, pull the covers over my head and sleep until I had a new life. Force of habit, however, caused me to listen to the one message that had been left even though I didn't recognize the number stored in caller I.D.

"Maya?" an unfamiliar man's voice spoke my name. "It's your father."

I almost dropped the phone. I pressed the message repeat button even though I hadn't finished listening to it the first time. Had this voice really said what I thought

I'd heard? I listened to the message from the beginning. "Maya? This is your father. Lottie told me she saw you. I got your number from her. If you'd like to talk to your old man, give me a call. I'd love to talk to you." I pressed the repeat button three more times before I believed I had received a phone call from my dad.

---

The sun was already up when I woke up the next morning. I looked at the paper where I had written the number my father had recited. "Ohm, ohm, ohm." The phone only rang once before it was picked up. A man's voice, still groggy with sleep, sounded on the other end. I looked at the clock, something I should have done before I dialed. It was not yet seven. That equated to sleeping late for me, but it was still early for most people. Hanging up the phone crossed my mind but since everyone seemed to have caller I.D., anonymity was a thing of the past. I didn't want him to think I was some kind of nut-case whack-a-doodle. "I'm sorry to call so early," I began.

"Maya?"

How'd he know? How could he possibly know that it was me?

"Baby-girl is that you?"

"Yes." That's all I could think to say. The tears that streamed down my face tasted salty as they ran into my mouth. I searched for a tissue.

"Baby, you ain't never got to apologize for calling me. Time don't matter. Understand that?"

"Yes."

"Since we're both awake, can I buy you breakfast?"

"Sure." It seemed I was only capable of one word sentences. I wrote down the address of the restaurant he suggested and promised I'd see him in about an hour.

# Chapter 42 – Tony

I might as well get up because there was no way I was going to fall back asleep. I pushed aside my thoughts of Maya. I needed to stay focused on Brenda and the baby. They needed me. I said another quick prayer of thanks that the surgery had gone well. The doc said my niece should have a complete recovery.

In a few minutes my place was filled with the smell of freshly brewed coffee. I took a sip and sighed. Hospital visiting hours didn't start for another few hours so I contemplated joining the joggers I watched from my fifth story window. A brisk morning run along the lake might help me clear my head. Maybe I had been too hard on Maya. Maybe I should have given Brenda the opportunity to accept or reject Maya's gift. Oh well. I'd messed up my chances with her for sure now. I chuckled when I heard Brenda's voice in my head. "You never had a chance with her anyway." Maybe, maybe not.

A seagull sailed across the horizon and landed on a pile of rocks on the other side of the lake that was as smooth as silk today. Sometimes Lake Michigan was so choppy you could get seasick just looking out the window. That was one of the main things I loved about my condo, the view of the lake. Further north than the beautiful folks on the Gold Coast, but right at the dividing line where Lake Shore Drive became Marine Drive, and the price of condos dropped considerably, but still appreciated nicely.

It had taken me almost a year before I found this place, but it was worth the wait and the effort I'd put into it. I'd ripped out all the carpeting and restored the hardwood floors myself. They were gorgeous. I patched and painted the walls. A couple of buddies from work and I renovated the kitchen. And we did it right, new cabinets, granite countertops, top of the line appliances, a tumbled marble back splash that a chick I was dating, Susan, helped me to pick out.

Our relationship hadn't survived but I would be eternally grateful for her legacy that lived on in my kitchen. I never knew there were so many little decisions that had to made, like light fixtures and draw pulls and on and on and on. Susan knew her stuff when it came to interior decorating. She subscribed to every shelter magazine on the planet and her television was permanently stuck on HGTV.

I know she thought she was going to become the lady of the house and that's the reason she worked so hard helping me out. When we first started going out it looked like she had the potential to become the future Mrs. Anthony Jackson. I wanted to find a woman with whom I could settle down and share my life. I didn't need three bedrooms for just me. I wanted a place where a couple of people could feel comfortable, each have his or her own space, and still have room for a baby, at least for a few years, until we bit the bullet and left city life behind in exchange for the suburbs, a big yard and better school systems. But the more time Susan and I spent together, the more I realized she wasn't the one.

She had a degree in business administration and worked for a major company as their national sales training manager but she hated it. She wanted to be an interior decorator but said she couldn't quit her current gig until she got married. That turned me off. I understood not cutting off the money flow. That's being smart. But I couldn't understand why she couldn't get the ball started. Take a class in the evenings or on the weekend. Even work part-time at a furniture store that offered interior design services, get some on-the-job training. Do something that took her in that direction since she was so sure that's where she wanted to go.

Then it hit me. The chick was lazy. The girl could talk the talk but I didn't ever see her walking the walk, even after she got married. I could see her quitting her current job. But I didn't see her taking the initiative of ever getting another one, in interior design or anywhere else. For me it wasn't about the money. It was about her character.

I poured myself another cup of coffee. Maybe Brenda was right. It wasn't the women I was dating. It was me. Every one I met had some issue. The girls from high school had been too ghetto. The women I worked with at UPS weren't sophisticated enough. The career women were ... too interested in their careers.

The ringing of the telephone startled me. Who'd be calling me this early in the morning? Oh shit. I raced to the phone. My heart pounded. I prayed it wasn't the hospital, that this wasn't a repeat of a morning when I picked up the receiver and it was someone from the

*Surrender to Love*

hospital telling me my mother had just passed. "Yes?"

"Tony?"

My heart slowed to a normal beat. "Monica?"

"Yeah," she said over the phone.

"How was Jamaica?" I asked. This was a surprise. A pleasant surprise. I didn't think I'd ever hear from her again.

"When you've been on one of these company incentive trips, you've been on them all." We were both silent. I wondered if she was thinking what I was thinking, that we ended a relationship that felt very special over something that, in the end, didn't really matter.

"How's Brenda?"

I told her about the baby. To me she sounded genuinely concerned. "Want some company before you go to the hospital?"

I thought for a second and nodded. "Yeah, I would. That would be nice. Very nice."

## Chapter 43 – Maya

I checked the address of the diner against the slip of paper in my hand. This was it. Ruthie's Pancake and Waffle House. I turned off the car but couldn't force myself to open the door. "Ohm, ohm, ohm." I felt my blood pressure rising. That would be a great first impression ... if I walked into the restaurant and passed out. But this wasn't my first time meeting my father. Hadn't Lottie said I had once been the apple of his eye?

Before he said anything I recognized the man walking toward me as my father. I knew that not just because he was the same shade of brown as me or that his hair was thick and black and wavy like my own; I knew because when I looked into his eyes I saw myself.

"Maya?" he asked. "You okay?"

I nodded, took a deep breath and opened the door.

*Surrender to Love*

We stood facing one another. Cousin Lottie was right. He was a good looking man. I wondered whether he had thrown on this ensemble for me or if he always looked this pulled together. My guess was a little of both. He probably always looked dapper like a Kweisi Mfume or Kofi Annan. *And* he'd probably added a little something special for our date. I wondered if he felt as awkward as I did. Should I hug him? Should I shake his hand? Standing before me was a person with whom I shared fifty percent of my DNA but I didn't even know his last name.

"You look like your mother," he finally said.

"Everyone says that." I couldn't think of anything else to add.

"Hungry?"

"I can always eat."

He chuckled as though I'd said something surprisingly witty. Maybe he was nervous, too. He touched my elbow and I fell in step next to him as we walked into the diner. I thought it was my imagination that a hush fell over the room that was surprisingly crowded. But when he announced to the entire place, "This is my daughter, Maya," I knew that people really had stopped what they were doing to watch our entrance. Folks smiled and nodded. He must be a regular here.

A black woman who weighed at least three hundred pounds waddled over to our table. "Hey, baby," she said to me. "I'm Ruthie. You want some coffee?"

I nodded. Without asking she filled my father's cup.

"So you a coffee drinker, too?"

"Yeah, I am."

"Ain't nothing like a good cup of hot coffee to get your day started off right."

I smiled and nodded. He looked at me without speaking. I blushed.

"You ready to order something or you all want to sit

a spell?" asked Ruthie.

I looked to my father for guidance. "I got all day," he said, tossing the question back to me.

"Sit a spell," I answered.

Ruthie went back to her seat at the counter.

"I'm sorry about your momma."

"Thanks." I had wondered if he knew my mother was dead. I assumed Lottie had told him.

"You sure put her away nice."

"How would you know?" I made the statement before thinking how rude it sounded. But in a life that had spanned sixty years, less than twenty people attended her funeral. And half of them were friends of mine. The crowd wasn't big enough for a stranger to have gotten lost in it.

He shook his head and sighed. "I thought about it but I didn't know if she would have wanted that." He sipped his coffee. "That's one of the few decisions I ever regretted." He shrugged. "I stopped by the funeral home before the ceremony to pay my respects."

Even my monosyllabic vocabulary was lost. I couldn't think of a single thing to say.

"So, how you making it? She told me you guys was close."

His question surprised me for two reasons. One, that he and my mother were still in communication with one another. Two, because she said that we were close. "You and momma still talked on a regular basis?" I asked him.

My father chuckled and sipped his coffee. "Yeah, that woman." He shook his head and smiled. "I've known a lot of women in my day but after God made Sissy Latimer he broke the mold."

I wasn't sure if he meant that statement as a compliment or a slam. "I'm okay," I finally said when he looked to me for a response to his inquiry on my well being.

*Surrender to Love*

"I kept hoping one day you'd pop over when I was there but..." His words trailed off. We both knew that never happened.

A thousand question fragments swam around in my head but none formulated a complete thought that I could articulate.

"Let me show you something." He dug into his jacket and pulled out his wallet. He opened it to my second grade school photo. My two front teeth were missing and my hair was parted down the middle into two fat ponytails. "That's my favorite picture of you."

I looked from the photograph to him then back to the photograph. That really was me. My father carried a picture of me in his wallet. I repeated that over and over to myself. My father had a picture of me. That he carried in his wallet.

"You had just brung them home when I came by your momma's house. They was laying out on the table."

That was our tradition. Every year when my school pictures arrived my mother cut the pictures apart and put the most recent eight-by-ten in a frame that sat on the end table in the living room and a wallet-sized image in the frame she'd keep on her bedroom dresser. The rest of the pictures I would return to school. I asked her why she hadn't put up my new picture in the bedroom that year. When she didn't answer, I assumed it was because she didn't want to wake up and see my snaggled-toothed smile. I thought that year she had only purchased a big picture. Now I knew. My father had taken the wallet-sized.

"Look at the rest of them."

I flipped through the pictures in his wallet. Each was of me. There were three in all. Three pictures of me. My second and sixth grade school pictures and a Polaroid of my high school graduation. I held the photo out to him.

"You were there?"

He nodded and accepted a refill of his coffee. "I was

there. I was so proud when they called your name and you marched across that stage."

This time I smiled at my father's imitation of how I had strutted. He had been there.

"I started to come over but ..." He shrugged. "I didn't want to make it hard on you. I know your momma needed you to be for her. Just for her. She didn't want to share you. She felt like you was all she ever had."

I sat with my cup suspended in the air halfway between the table and my lips. He understood what it had taken a lifetime for me to comprehend about my mother.

"It was hard on a girl like your momma. Raised without no parents. No brothers and sisters." My mother had been taken in by Cousin Lottie's mother when her mother died in child birth and her father abdicated the responsibility of raising a girl child alone. With half a dozen kids already, by half as many men, one more child in the house didn't matter.

We were both silent. Each of us understood the loneliness of growing up without the family for which we longed.

"Besides, she was still mad at me. But shit, I didn't know." He looked at me for understanding then called the waitress. I guess we'd lost our opportunity to be served by Miss Ruthie when the only other waitress in the place came to take our order. Though I wasn't hungry I ordered a couple of scrabbled eggs and toast.

"Shit, how was I supposed to know?"

He didn't give me a chance to ask him *know what?* before he continued. "I didn't know when your momma got that job with the city and you all moved into that little house she had made up this whole new version of her life. I knew she deserved a fresh start, that's for damned sure. She was too smart to be scrubbing somebody else's toilets all her life."

Amen to that.

"So when I heard the city was looking for women for

*Surrender to Love*

this *Fresh Start* program, of course, I told her about it."

"You told her?"

"Back in the day wasn't nothing happening in the city that I didn't know about." My father stuck the end of his toast into the yolk from his egg. "Thing's different now, but back then, I hung with all them cats. Wasn't too much difference between the councilmen and the criminals, if you know what I mean?" I could see him as a mover-and-shaker in the black Chicago political scene.

"I'd heard she'd gotten in, so when I bumped into her I was expecting a thank you or something, you know? Nothing much 'cause I knew how your mother was, but I thought I'd get a little something."

I nodded. We both knew how my mother was.

"And Lord have mercy, I know that's your momma so I don't mean no disrespect but that was one good looking woman."

"Yes, she was." It broke my heart to speak of her in the past tense.

"So when I saw her, she had on this sleeveless cotton dress tied at the waist."

He still remembered what she was wearing? He loved her. He loved her as much as she loved him.

"She was looking so good I couldn't help myself. I went up and grabbed her and kissed her smack on the mouth."

We both smiled. I imagined how my prim and proper mother would react to a public display of affection like that. But then again, maybe I didn't know anything.

"That woman always could get me all riled up." He slathered jelly on his biscuit and bit into the dough as though it had insulted his momma.

"Well, your momma tried to pretend like she was all I-don't-need-no-body but I could tell." My father looked at me above the rim of his coffee cup.

"Well, this man jumps up in my face like he's going to defend her. Like I'm molesting her or something, you know what I'm saying?"

When did this happen? Twenty years ago? And still my father was incensed at the memory of it.

"Well, I tell him what me and my wife is doing ain't none of his god damned business."

I put down my fork when I realized I held it in mid air. I folded my hands in my lap. Until my father finished his story, eating and listening were two tasks it was too difficult for me to simultaneously master.

"Then this mother fucker says, your wife? And I say yes my mother-fucking wife. We never got married, not legal, cause she didn't want to, but it was common-law, you know?"

Again, I nodded.

"Well he looks at her like he wants some kind of explanation. She standing there looking down at her shoes like her eyeballs been glued to the ground. So I ask him who the fuck is he?" My father stopped talking. He put down his own fork and looked at me. "He was the pastor of her new church. Even though I think the nigger was trying to do more than save her soul. You know what I mean?"

He was jealous. After all these years, he was still jealous.

"Well, she had told him she was a widow. That her husband died when you was a little bitty baby girl."

My father shook his head as if he still couldn't explain why he reacted the way he did. "I don't know why but that pissed the hell out of me. I called that man everything but a child a God. And your momma just stood there looking like I was the monster from the black lagoon. Girl, I was hot." He continued to shake his head. "Your momma was the only person I ever knew my whole damned life who could get me to completely lose my cool."

Because he loved her. That's why she made him react that way. Because he loved her. And she loved him. And no one had taught either of them how grown up people were supposed to love one another.

"Next time I went by the house she wouldn't let me in. Told me I had shamed her. That she'd stopped going to church 'cause she was too embarrassed to show her face. I felt bad but not that bad. Ain't church supposed to be the place filled with forgiveness?"

So that's why we stopped going to that church. When we first moved to the house, for the first five Sundays we visited a different church until we settled on Greater Abyssinia. She only had two more new members classes to complete before we'd become members. I was going to be baptized and she would be invited into the church family through Christian experience. But one Sunday we just stopped going.

The first Sunday we missed I thought a miracle had happened and she'd forgotten that it was Sunday. The next week when we didn't go, I asked her if everything was all right. When the third Sunday rolled around and still we didn't get up and start getting ready for church, she told me we were taking a little break, that we could study the bible at home. "Don't the bible say wherever two or more are gathered together in his name, you at church?" she asked me.

If she said it I assumed it must be true so I said, "Yes."

"Then we at church every day."

And that was it. We stopped going to church. And I stopped asking why. Now twenty-plus years later, I had my answer.

I handed my plate to the waitress who'd come to collect the dirty dishes. "You didn't like the eggs?"

"No. I mean yes. I liked them. I'm just not very hungry."

The waitress nodded in understanding. "Ain't everyday you meet up with your daddy. He been looking forward to this day for a long time." She patted me on the shoulder then lifted the tray filled with dirty dishes.

"So," he said.

"So," I repeated.

"Tell me about yourself."

I wasn't sure where to begin. Before I could start, he cut me off.

"Let me just say this first, okay?"

I wondered what he was going to tell me now. That the woman I thought was my mother wasn't really my mother? Cousin Lottie wasn't really my cousin? He wasn't really a human being? He was actually an alien from another planet? At this point nothing would surprise me.

"I don't know what your momma has told you about me." He looked at me to see if I wanted to say anything. He grunted and concluded, "Nothing probably."

I didn't respond.

"It don't matter. That's all right. I never did none of the stuff I did 'cause I wanted credit for it. I gave your momma money to buy your school clothes when I had it. I helped her out with your college tuition when I could. I was just getting the business started so I wasn't making no big money but I had started to do all right."

I wondered how my mother had been able to pay my college expenses. I had scholarships for tuition and room and board but there were still travel expenses, books, clothes ...

"I knew the little bit of change I was throwing her wasn't shit in comparison to what she was doing. I just did what I could when I could."

I understood. I really did.

"Well, baby, whatever she said or whatever she didn't say, it don't matter at all."

I silently thanked him for letting me off the hook. I didn't want to tell him she had never told me any of this. That she let me grow up thinking my father neither knew nor cared about me.

He reached out for my hand. His nails were buffed to a soft sheen. "I ain't going to lie to you. Ain't no reason for me to."

I hoped I was prepared for what he was about to say. But I knew if I needed support he wouldn't let me fall.

"I have known a lot of women in my life, black, white, Hispanic, Asian. If the bitch had a pussy I been with her, you hear what I'm saying?"

I nodded.

"But this is the God's honest truth. You," he said and looked directly into my eyes, eyes that looked exactly like his own, "You," he repeated and squeezed my fingers, "And your crazy-assed momma are the only women I've ever truly loved."

Like the images I'd seen of glaciers tumbling down into the ocean, thawed by waters heated from global warming, I felt myself implode. My father loved me. He always had. And that was enough.

# Chapter 44 – Tony

When I opened the door Monica held out a bag of bagels.

"I knew you'd already have coffee."

She looked good. And felt even better as I encircled her in my arms and squeezed. When she pulled back, tears shimmered in her eyes but she quickly blinked them away. I couldn't believe my girl was getting sentimental. It was good seeing her softer side.

"I've missed talking to you," she said.

"Me, too," I said. But with everything that had been happening I hadn't missed her as much as I thought. I sliced a couple of bagels and generously spread butter on them before placing them on the griddle to brown. I poured her a cup of coffee and scooped in two heapings of sugar. She knew I didn't believe in artificial sweeteners. The chemicals in them could do more harm than the calories from the sugar. After pouring in a generous helping of cream, not half-and-half, cream, I handed the cup to her. She took a sip and sighed. "Perfect."

I felt her watching me while I prepared myself another cup.

"You looking at my ass?" I teased.

"Yes," she said without hesitation. "And wondering how long we need to make small talk before I can use my womanly wiles and lure you into bed." She accepted the toasted bagel I handed her. That was another thing I liked about her. She was straight-up, no chaser. I had no grounds upon which to be angry with her. She had never played games with me. She was always who she purported herself to be, a strong, fine-ass sister.

It must have been very sunny in Jamaica because her honey-brown complexion had taken on a slightly darker hue. She looked really good. I felt that familiar stirring in my groin. She wasn't wearing a bra. And I knew that she knew I would notice. She was teasing me. And it was working. When she set down her coffee cup I assumed she was coming over to me but she rummaged through the tote bag she'd brought in with her and pulled out a small box tied with a silver bow. If our genders were reversed, when she handed it to me I would have thought there was an engagement ring inside.

"What's this?" I took out a silver locket with a photograph of a puppy.

"He's the pick of the litter from a cattle and collie farm in east-butt-fuck-Kansas. The breeder's holding him until I let her know if we'd like him. What do you think?"

I never had a dog as a kid but I'd always wanted one. We had talked about it once. I saw me and my pooch playing Frisbee on fall afternoons while the kids stomped through the yard disrupting the piles of leaves

I had just raked. In my dog-fantasy, my dog would be a combination of Nana, the dog from Peter Pan and Astro, the dog from the Jetsons. I imagined him keeping an eye on the kids while we vacationed at the beach, herding them away from the lapping waves when they played too close to the water's edge. Then he'd herd them off for their naps while their mom and I had lunch in an adjoining suite.

"You want to get a dog?" I asked Monica.

"I want *us* to get a dog," she said. "As a compromise." She took the coffee cup from my hand and set it on the counter. "What do you think?" I couldn't answer because I was distracted by the sight of her unbuttoning her blouse. She slipped my hand, still warm from the heat of the coffee cup, onto her breasts. My mouth automatically closed around one of her nipples. I heard her sigh. Or was that me?

"I've missed you, Tony. I've missed you so much."

As if we were enacting the final scene from *An Officer and a Gentleman*, I scooped her up and carried her into my bedroom. Monica, who normally liked being in control, loved for me to take charge in the boudoir. She lay on her back and waited for me to undress her. As I peeled her clothes off, one piece at a time, I felt her muscles twitching with desire. I buried my face between her legs. Her orgasm came so quickly and with such force we both laughed when she tapped me on the head to signal she was done. Or at least she thought she was done. Before the morning was over we'd both come two more times.

We lay on the edge of the bed wrapped in one another's arms. "So what do you say?" she asked.

"About what?" I wasn't normally the type who rolled over and fell asleep after sex but there are always exceptions. And this morning was one of them. I pulled her body close to mine. She felt so warm.

"The puppy?"

*Surrender to Love*

"Let's talk about it later." I closed my eyes but felt Monica sit up. "Where you going?"

"Shower. Want to join me?"

Her body looked extremely inviting but I couldn't get another erection if my life depended on it. I shook my head. "I'm going to take a quick nap."

"I have to let the breeder know before noon."

"I don't know, Monica. I thought you couldn't have dogs in your condo?"

"I can't. He'd have to live here."

"He would have to live here or the two of you would have to live here?"

She stopped looking through her tote bag. "He would live here but I'd come over or you could bring him when you come to my place."

"Why?"

"Why what? So we could spend time together. Like a family," she added.

I sat up. "A man, a woman and a dog don't make a family. A man, a woman and a dog make a couple with a pet."

She bit her lip and sighed. "I'm trying, Tony. Can I get credit for that?"

I got up and wrapped my arms around her. "I know you are babe. You're right, Monica. You're right."

She stepped back so that she could look me in the eyes. "What does that mean?"

"It means you've got the right to want what you want."

"You really mean that?"

I nodded. I did mean it.

She wrapped her arms around me. This time I pulled back.

"And I've got the right to want what I want. I may want a dog one day, but that'll be a family decision. Something me and my wife will decide with input from our kids, dependent on how old they are when we decide our family is ready for a pet."

"I see."

"I'm going for a run," I said. I slipped on a pair of jogging shorts. "Just let yourself out, okay?"

She nodded again.

"And leave your keys on the counter when you go."

"No problem."

I knew I'd never see her perfect pair of boobs again.

# Chapter 45 – Tony

Brenda sat in the rocking chair of the hospital nursery while I paced back and forth like a nervous dad. My niece, Deanna Antonia, was coming home today. I'd work the rest of the week then take off the next four to help Brenda out. She had always been squeamish about bandages and blood, but the doctors said the incision in Deanna's head would be healed in another couple of weeks. We were blessed.

"When are they bringing me my baby? I want to get the hell up out of here."

"Relax."

"Isn't that advice you ought to be giving yourself?"

"Don't start."

"Call her."

"Call who?"

*Surrender to Love*

"Don't play ignorant with me." Brenda rocked back and forth. "I haven't seen you mopping around like this since I was in the second grade and you had a crush on Lucretia Gilmore."

"I didn't have a crush on Lucretia Gilmore's fat ass."

She stopped rocking and stared at me. "The hell you didn't," she said. "She'd come over to baby-sit so you could go do something else and we couldn't even play Barbie without you hanging around trying to butt in." Brenda imitated a teenage boy's voice. "I'll be Ken. You need me to play Ken? I can be Ken."

I laughed out loud. My sister was a certified nut.

"You're attracted to these women because they're strong and independent, then when they don't act the way *you* think they should, you dump them."

"That's not true."

She gave me a sister-girl-no-you-didn't look. "If you want an independent woman, don't get mad at her for acting independently. It ain't fair to fault a person for being who you knew they were in the first place."

I was silent as Brenda's counsel sank in. That's the same thing Monica had said. Maybe they had a point. Maybe.

The nurse walked into the nursery with a pink bundle cradled in her arms. Brenda reached for her baby who had already gained almost two full pounds.

"Call her," she said, still looking down at her daughter. "Call Maya. I know you want to."

"I thought you didn't think she was the one."

She shrugged. "What the hell do I know?"

"True that." I grinned at my baby sister. She looked more beautiful than I had ever seen her as she sat there with her baby nestled against her chest.

"People didn't think Dean was the one for me." Her voice almost broke but she continued, "But even knowing what I know, I wouldn't have done anything any different."

The baby gurgled and waved her hands in the air.

"She looks like Dean, don't she?" asked Brenda.

I nodded but at this point she didn't look like much of anyone to me.

"Call her," Brenda repeated. "Life's too short for bullshit. Call Maya."

## Chapter 46 – Tony

I pushed my two-wheeler across the marble foyer. All evidence that Narcisco Industries had ever existed had vanished, replaced by Musikiwa International.

"I've only been gone a week and everything's changed," I said to the guards at the security desk when I stopped to check in.

"Yeah and you missed it," volunteered the oldest one.

"Missed what?"

"You know that new black woman that started a few weeks ago at Narcisco?"

"The one that thought her shit didn't stink?" added the youngest of the three, LaQuicia. I never understood why Maya rubbed her the wrong way. Must be a female thing, like Brenda and Monica.

"She was always nice to me," added the one who seemed slightly retarded.

"The bitch was fake. F. A. K. E."

"I don't think so."

"What the hell do you know?"

"You mean Maya?" I interjected. That argument could go on all day.

"Yeah, Ms. Maya."

"What happened?"

LaQuicia leaned forward and lowered her voice so that I was forced to move closer. "I don't know exactly what she did but we had to escort her from the building."

I looked to the other two women for confirmation. They nodded.

"Some tall ugly woman who looked like Miss Hathaway from the *Beverly Hillbillies* told her to never come back. Her ass was fired. Cha-ching." LaQuicia motioned as though something had been catapulted through the air. "Gone."

Once again the nodding of the other guards' verified the accuracy of LaQuicia's version of events.

"They may not have made her go home but they sure as hell made her get her ass from up in here."

The three women chuckled at that old joke as if they'd never heard it before.

# Chapter 47 – Maya

For the first time in almost thirty years my father and I hugged one another. Standing by my car, my dad kissed me on the cheek and said he'd see me later. We'd made plans for him to come to my place for dinner Saturday night, just the two of us. Neither of us was ready to share one another with the other folks in our lives.

He had leveraged his connections to start his own business, a security agency, and won some of the most lucrative contracts in the city. Coincidentally, he provided the security guards for the building that was home to Narcisco Industries, now Musikiwa International. Throughout my life my father's presence had been all around me; I had just never known it. We

*Surrender to Love*

still had so much to learn about each other, a lifetime of catching up. And Lord willing, we still had plenty of time to get it done.

I cruised through the neighborhood surrounding Ruthie's Pancake and Waffle House. It seemed vaguely familiar. Then it dawned on me. Ruthie's wasn't far from the skating rink to which Tony had taken me. Just as that realization came to me, I drove past it. Three of the letters in the neon sign were still out and another blinked on and off. I checked my rear view mirror, crossed two lanes of traffic and pulled my car to a stop in front. The night I'd come here with Tony I hadn't noticed the small sign printed on card stock and stuck in the front window of a dilapidated old house next door. *The North Avenue Project*. This was the place Tony told me about. This was the place Brenda's husband had started.

A teenage girl, her belly swollen to the size of a large watermelon, answered the security buzzer and told me to come in. Two little black children played with a toy stove and refrigerator that looked as if they hijacked them from someone's trash pile. An attractive African-American woman who looked like she was in her late twenties walked over to me and the teenager.

"Honey, you're supposed to find out who it is before you buzz them in. That's the purpose of a security system," she said.

"But I seen her get out of a Benz," the girl responded as if her logic made all the sense in the world.

"What's that supposed to prove? Bad people don't always look bad."

"All right." The girl looked down at her feet.

"Go on."

"I promise I'm not a bad guy," I said. I smiled at the woman. I hoped the girl knew it hadn't been my intent to get her in trouble. She rolled her eyes at me.

"Sorry about that." The woman held out her hand to

me. "My name's Allison Graham. I'm the center director. I didn't mean any offense to you. I'm just working with these kids ..." Allison let the sentence trail off. I could imagine the variety of ways in which she could have finished it.

"Hi, I'm Maya Latimer."

She stopped me and walked over to another little girl who had started wailing at the top of her lungs. "It's all right sweetie," Allison said over and over again. "Niece, get over here and take care of your baby." The teenager who'd opened the door shuffled back into the room. I wondered if Allison had meant the statement literally or figuratively. Was she pregnant with another child when she was only a child herself? The pregnant girl tended to the little girl.

"Sorry about all that. How may I help you?" Allison asked me as the little girl's sobs subsided. Two toddlers stood behind her. They peeped around her legs watching me as if I were an exhibit at the zoo.

"Lexus, Duvall, get away from Miss Allison and let her take care of her business," shouted the pregnant teenager.

When the children ran back to play, I cleared my throat and said, "I wondered if you needed volunteers." Now that I was standing here I realized how strange this must seem. I debated how much of my story to go into and decided though all of the events of the past week were pertinent, none were appropriate to share. I finally shrugged and simply said, "I have some extra time on my hands right now and thought I should put it to good use."

Allison motioned for me to follow her. As we walked through the house, every room begged for repair. She stooped over and picked up a big wheel that blocked the entrance to the kitchen.

"You need help, don't you?"

She looked at me with an expression that conveyed the same meaning as the words she finally spoke.

"Look around. Do you have to ask?"

I wasn't sure whether the question was rhetorical or if she expected an answer.

"We definitely need help."

She stopped at the kitchen sink and washed her hands before she stirred a pot of turnip greens that simmered on the stove. I couldn't remember the last time I'd had greens. Not since my mother died. My stomach growled. Now, I wished I had eaten something at Ruthie's.

"Of course we need help." She grunted. "We need more than help. We need a miracle." She chuckled to herself. I stood in the middle of the kitchen and watched as another women came in carrying a load of laundry.

"Smelling good in here," Allison said to the woman.

"Got to keep our girls well fed." The woman smiled and revealed a front grill of sterling silver.

Allison motioned for me to go through the kitchen door. We stepped out onto a small landing that could be called a patio if one used labels generously. More children played on the swing and sliding board set up in the back yard that was about the size of my bedroom. Another section served as a basketball court, non-regulation.

"So what is this place?"

She laughed and shrugged. "Good question." She waved to one of the little boys on the swing. "I like to think of it as an oasis; a safe haven."

I looked at the peeling paint on the house's exterior, the stairs that needed to be torn down and rebuilt, the playground equipment that appeared about as old as our combined ages. As if she'd read my thoughts, she said, "Might not look like much to you but when a mother finds out her boyfriend is her daughter's baby-daddy and they're all living together and she has nowhere else to go, this place looks pretty darn good."

I silently agreed.

"We provide room and board, have a social worker who volunteers here a few days a month. Once a month a couple of physicians have a kind of a free clinic."

"That's all?" I hadn't intended to sound so judgmental.

"I wish we could do more but you do what you can until you can do better."

I watched two more teenage girls come through the back gate. Both were pregnant. They waved to Allison who waved back.

"These girls are just babies themselves."

Allison nodded.

"I can't believe their parents would put them out just because they made a mistake."

"Let me get one thing straight."

I stood at attention. My heart raced. I knew from the tone of her voice that I had crossed an invisible line but I wasn't sure exactly what my offense had been.

"These babies may be unplanned. They may even be unwanted. But they're never a mistake. God don't make no mistakes."

I wondered if that's how my mother felt when she found out she was pregnant with me? My father told me when she'd first informed him that she was pregnant he offered to take her to a guy he knew who performed abortions. Thirty-three years later, he apologized to me for that. "I don't think she ever really trusted me after that," he'd said. "That's why she wouldn't marry me. She didn't want me to have no kind of legal rights to you."

Like my mother's need to protect me from harm, real or perceived, I sensed Allison's instincts to protect these kids was strong. "I'm sorry," I said. "I didn't mean any offense."

She smiled. I saw her body relax. "I'm sorry, too. I'm just a little sensitive when it comes to my girls. I didn't mean to come off so harsh."

*Surrender to Love*

"Until a friend of mine mentioned it, I never knew this place even existed."

"A friend?"

"Yeah," I said. "Tony Jackson."

"So you must be the hottie the boys were telling us Tony was hanging out with at the skating rink."

I blushed. It felt good that the boys had thought enough of our meeting to mention me.

Allison waved back to the same little boy who laughed at himself when he fell off the swing. She took a closer look at me. "I was surprised Tony had a woman with him. He's really careful about who he exposes these kids to. You must be special."

I was flattered but also detected a note of warning in her voice. She turned her attention from the kids on the playground and looked directly at me. "Lord knows we need all the help we can get, but one thing these children don't need is another person to walk out on them. We need helping hands but we also need money."

Less than a week ago money was the only thing I would have thought to offer but now I said, "I need to do more than write a check this time. I can do that, too," I assured her. I rubbed my hand over my heart. "But *I* want to help. *I* need to do something."

Allison nodded.

"Believe it or not I'm a pretty good cook," I volunteered. "Or I could do fund raising or public relations. I could do laundry, even. That's the one household chore I really enjoy. I like making order out of chaos."

"Why does that not surprise me?"

My smile faded. Was she making fun of me?

"That wasn't a slam." She laughed. "It's just that you remind me of myself."

I resisted the impulse to ask her "How?" I'd put my foot in my mouth enough times during this visit.

"Remember Hurricane Katrina?"

"Of course."

"Well, while that was happening, I was sitting at home in my plush thirty-eight hundred square foot loft condo watching those poor black people who were already living in dilapidated, substandard housing lose what little they had and I just couldn't get those images out of my head."

I understood. I had resolved my feelings of despair by sending a five hundred dollar check to the Red Cross. Then I stopped watching or reading the news coverage. It was too much. I felt a renewed empathy for the people as we talked about it right now. If I couldn't stand to look at it, how had they managed to live through it? How were they coping in the aftermath of it? It was time for me to do something else.

"Then I started thinking about the people living right here, in Chicago, right in the neighborhood where I grew up, some of them living in the same conditions or worse than the people in New Orleans."

I looked around the community in which the North Avenue Project resided. If this neighborhood were televised without captions it would be difficult to distinguish it from war-torn Iraq.

"I was going to volunteer with an existing agency doing this kind of work but there weren't any, at least none that I could find, then I talked to a friend I grew up with."

"Dean?"

"Yeah." She nodded. "And one thing led to another. I took a year leave of absence from my job. I was at a point where I was feeling pretty burned out with corporate America, anyway. It was a good time to take a break. We pooled a few pennies together to buy this house."

"And the North Avenue project was born." I finished the story for her.

"If we don't help each other, who else will? Lord knows, don't nobody else care about poor black people.

"And half the time we don't care about ourselves."

"Half the time?" she asked. "Girlfriend, you must be an optimist."

We both chuckled at the sad reality.

"Hey," said the pregnant girl who had answered the door for me. "Mind if I sit out here for a minute? It's hot as heck in the house."

I moved over to make room for her.

"Take my seat," said Allison. "Let me go check on those kids. It's too quiet in there."

We nodded and watched her disappear back into the kitchen.

"Them some bad-ass shoes," said the pregnant girl.

"Thanks." My father wasn't the only one who'd put forth a little extra effort to look good for our breakfast meeting.

"What size you is?"

"Six." I watched the girl look from the shoes on my feet to her own. "Want to try them on?"

Her face lit up like a Christmas tree. "Can I?"

I slipped off the pair of shoes that would probably pay the mortgage on the North Avenue Project house for a couple of months. I watched her prance back and forth in the high-heeled pumps like a kid playing dress up. "They look good on you."

She sat back down and rubbed her protruding belly. "I'll be glad when this little nigger drop." She looked at me. "Don't that feel good?"

"I don't know."

"You ain't got kids?"

I shook my head. "Not yet. I haven't met the right guy."

"I love my kids but sometimes I wish I'd waited."

I shrugged and said, "Sometimes I wish I hadn't."

The girl rubbed her feet. She looked like she wore about a seven and a half. I was surprised she had been able to stuff them into my shoes.

"I thought my baby's daddy was the one. Said we'd

get a place together. He was gonna stop slinging and get a real job. I can't believe I fell for that shit. Twice."

"You're not the first girl to believe the lies the man she's in love with is telling her."

"I bet you wouldn't."

"I did." I admitted the secret not even my two best friends knew. "I dated a married man for almost two years." Lillian and Donna knew Deuce was an asshole, but they didn't know he was a married asshole, a married to a white woman asshole, at that.

After making my confession I held my breath for several seconds and waited. Nothing happened. Thunder didn't rumble. Lighting didn't streak through the sky. I inhaled a deep cleansing breath. When I exhaled, I felt a sense of lightness, like when I first stopped eating red meat. I had spoken another truth and the earth hadn't opened up and devoured me.

"I really believed he was going to leave his wife." There I said it and no apparition appeared to condemn me to hell.

The girl shrugged. "He cheat on her, he'll cheat on you."

I put my shoes back on. "Took me awhile to figure that one out."

"Ain't nobody perfect."

If my mother and I had figured that out sooner, we both could have saved ourselves a lot of heartache and experienced a lot more joy.

"Ask God to forgive you, forgive yourself, then move the fuck on. That's what Miss Allison's always telling us. Well, not the fuck part. She don't cuss. Lest ways not in front of us." The girl picked at the chipped nail polish on her fingers. "It's hard, though."

"That's an understatement. But you know what? Stuff happens. You move on. More stuff happens. You still keep moving. That's what life's all about. Don't let anybody, even yourself, rob you of all the possibilities that are out there for you."

"I got two kids."
"I hope I'll be able to say that one day."
"You really think I ain't ruined my life?"
"Not even close."
"For real?"
"For real."

# Chapter 48 – Maya

My bed looked like a graveyard of discarded clothes. I pulled outfit after outfit from my closet, examined it, then threw it into the rejected pile. When I pulled out the Roberto Cavalli suit I had worn on the first day I met Tony, I knew that was it. The folks at Musikiwa International didn't know who they were messing with. I'm Maya Marie bi-aach!

# Chapter 49 – Maya

I sat across the desk from my two former bosses. "Maya, let me assure you we appreciate the contribution you've made to this organization," Carol began.

"You can save all that."

She nodded and pushed an envelope across the desk towards me. "Though this is an employment at will state, we've prepared a generous severance package."

I ripped it open and perused the contents. I wasn't interested in what she had to say. As the saying goes, *money talks, bullshit walks*. I pushed the envelope back toward her. "A week's pay for every year I've been here? You think after almost twelve years you can pay me off with twelve weeks pay?"

"Plus continuation of your benefits for another three months," she added.

I ignored her and addressed James Caplin. "How's the integration coming along?"

Carol motioned for him not to respond. She answered instead. "Wonderful. Our cultures are similar."

I interrupted her and spoke to James again. "Musikiwa International built their reputation on integrity."

"That's true," said Carol. "At one point there were other companies that were bigger, their product pipelines were more robust but Musikiwa was the company people could trust."

I cut her off again. My gaze was riveted on James Caplin.

"Honor above all else," she continued as if once she'd started the prepared spiel she couldn't stop until it had been completed.

"So I wonder how the senior executive team will feel about this?" I asked.

Carol stopped talking. James' eyes narrowed. They both watched as I fished a small tape recorder from my purse and pushed the play button. James' voice filled the office. "God, you're so tense. Relax." I watched the color drain from his face while Carol's turned a bright shade of red. "Everybody was really excited about the news today. But not half as excited as I am right now." Next, my voice sounded. "Get your hands off me." I watched James as he listened to himself on the tape. "Acquisition time can be a really tricky period in a company's history."

"Turn it off," he said.

Instead I pushed fast forward. "Why? Maybe Carol would like to know this." I added, "If she doesn't already." I pressed the play button and James' voice sounded again over the tape. "For a white guy I've been told I'm pretty well hung."

Carol gasped.

"What the fuck do you want?"

I pushed the stop button on the recorder. "Continuation of benefits for twelve months, company paid of course."

James nodded.

"A *months* pay for every year that I've been with the company."

"That's highly irregular," interrupted Carol.

"Fine." James glared at her. Her teeth clenched so tightly together it would take the jaws of life to pry them open.

"And a check for three hundred fifty thousand dollars."

Carol jumped up from her seat. "That's utterly ridiculous."

"Made out to the North Avenue Project." I looked directly at James, then Carol. "I've already spoken with an attorney. If there's anything that's ridiculous, it's that I'm letting you assholes off so cheap."

Carol sat down.

"Pay it."

"But Mr. Caplin."

"Just pay the fucking money." He shouted at her this time.

"Yes sir."

As if I were in the Musikiwa facility in Japan, I pressed my hands together and bowed to James and Carol. "*Konnichiwa.*"

There were two things I planned to accomplish today. One down, one to go.

# Chapter 50 – Maya

The UPS truck was still parked on the street. Good.

"Ohm. Ohm. Ohm." I chanted trying to lower the rapid beating of my pulse. I took a deep breath and strode toward the revolving doors. I checked my watch. Tony should be coming out any minute. My heart lurched when I saw the blonde-haired UPS driver walk through the revolving doors. "Where's Tony?" I know this guy probably thought I needed to get a life but I didn't care. I was on a mission.

"I can take your package, ma'am. They all end up at the same place."

I shook my head. My lower lip quivered. It hadn't occurred to me that he might not be at work today. I had to talk to him. I felt tears well up in my eyes.

"This isn't about package delivery, huh?"

Once again, I shook my head.

"He's working a later shift this week. He's probably at the station getting checked in."

I pulled into the employee parking lot outside the main UPS facility and rushed inside the doors marked *Employees Only*. Tony was surrounded by a group of other drivers.

"Tony!" I yelled.

Everyone turned around and stared at me.

"Maya?" He blinked twice as if he wanted to make sure I wasn't a mirage. "What's wrong?" He maneuvered his way past his coworkers and stood at my side.

"I'm sorry I didn't call you before I left for Japan. I should have made time. You were right."

He tried to steer me outside but I wouldn't budge.

"And I can cook. In fact I'm pretty good at it. I wanted to cook for you that night but my boss made me do this presentation and it got late and I didn't have time." I looked up at him. "I wanted to. I really wanted to." He needed to understand that it wasn't lack of desire that kept me from preparing a home cooked meal for him that night. In the spirit of full disclosure, I added, "I haven't done it in awhile so I might be a little rusty but it'll come back to me with practice." I was confident of that.

He stared at me without speaking. I could tell he was trying to understand what was happening. Like when you start watching a movie in the middle and you're trying to figure out what's transpired before you tuned in based on what's going on now. "You know I like to eat," he finally said. He guided me outside into the parking lot.

"And I do want babies, lots of them. Well, two of them, and I could probably be persuaded on three. And a husband."

He smiled.

"But not in that order," I clarified. I grasped his hand as if I was drowning and he were a life jacket.

"I want to be a husband and a father." He tried to pull me to his chest but I continued to resist him. I needed to look into his eyes. I needed to gauge whether I was getting through to him.

"I was going to call you tonight," he said. "That's why I couldn't believe it when I looked up and you were standing there. What happened at Narcisco? Or Musikiwa? Or whatever the name of your company is? Maggie said you don't work there anymore."

Three of his female coworkers followed us and stood a few feet behind him as if he might need protection from me.

I shook my head again. "I don't want to talk about Musikiwa. That's true, I don't work there anymore." For the first time I had spoken those words and didn't feel anything. Nothing. Not fear. Not shame. Nothing. Nada. Zilch. I didn't work there anymore but neither did most of the other people in the world. So what?"I don't want to talk about that." I stomped my foot like an angry two-year old.

"Okay, what do you want to talk about?"

"Us," I said, and fell silent. Suddenly, I felt shy.

"What about us?"

I looked up into his eyes. He ran his finger along the side of my cheek.

"You're the best man I've ever met. I'd be lucky to have you as my boyfriend."

"You know that's right," co-signed his coworker.

"As fine as he is," said the other one.

"Jaime Foxx ain't got nothin' on him." The three women laughed and gave one another high-fives.

I ignored them but Tony turned around and said, "Don't you all have anything better to do?"

"Hell no. This shit is better than the soaps."

"It's okay," I said. "I don't care if they stay. I want the

*Surrender to Love*

whole world to know that I ... I ..." I stuttered then began again, "That I could ..." I stopped.

"Could what?"

"I could fall in love with you."

I gazed up into his eyes. At last I allowed him to pull me to his chest. His arms felt so good around me.

"You silly goose. I've already fallen in love with you."

"Really?"

"Really." He kissed me on the top of my head.

"I love you too," I cried. "I should have said it first but I was scared."

"It's okay, babe." He put his arm around my shoulder. "Tony's here now. I'll take care of you."

I looked up at him and smiled. I shook my head. "No, we'll take care of each other," I corrected.

## Chapter 51 – Maya

I sat in the passenger seat of Tony's car while he went inside the UPS facility to clear his schedule. As his coworkers came out of the building, I saw them glancing over at me. It was a good thing Tony was taking some time off. Hopefully, by the time he got back to work, the hubbub about his crazy girlfriend would have died down. I could only imagine the teasing he was in for because of my erratic behavior.

But, oh well. No one was perfect all the time. And trying to be would wear you out. What was the advice, Niece, the pregnant girl from the North Avenue Project gave me? Ask God for forgiveness, forgive yourself, then move the fuck on. That's what I was doing. If making a fool of myself in front of people I neither knew nor cared about was what needed to happen for me to end up where I was, so be it. Sorry if I ruined their morning. They could get over it or dwell on it. I was done with it.

"I pulled your car around back," Tony said when he slipped into the driver's seat. "It'll be okay there. We'll come back later and pick it up, okay."

I hadn't even thought about my car being illegally parked. It was good having someone to watch my back.

"Let's go to my place," he said.

Once again, I nodded. I felt content to let him make all the decisions for a while. We were both silent as we drove to his place. I wondered what he was thinking but I was content to wait until he was ready to share. Me? My mind was clear.

When we pulled in front of his North side condo, I could tell he was proud of the place. He should be. It was gorgeous. It was about three times the size of my place. The address might not be as prestigious as mine but his place felt like a home. By comparison, my place felt like an upscale hotel suite.

"Want something to drink?"

"Coffee?" I suggested.

In a few moments the place was filled with the rich aroma of a dark roasted blend. Though his place had a bachelor pad feel to it, it was obvious he'd had some decorating assistance. I wondered if the help had come from a professional interior designer or one of his former lady friends, perhaps even a former lady friend who was a professional decorator. I had never employed the strategy Lillian used when she and Rick had gotten serious, but for the first time I felt the desire to. When Lillian became a regular overnight visitor at Rick's place, along with a toothbrush and other toiletries, she placed a giant box of tampons in the cabinet under the bathroom sink.

"Just in case there are some other women up in here, there ain't no way they won't get this message," she said when she held up the forty-eight count box of sanitary products. "The bottom bitch is in the house and she ain't no once-in-a-while visitor."

I planned to buy a box of tampons for under Tony's sink, as well as claim a dresser drawer and fill it with the sexiest lingerie I owned. If anybody ever did any snooping around, I wanted to make sure they found something. He was my man.

"Here you go," he said as he handed me a cup of coffee.

"Thanks." I patted the seat next to me on the sofa. Though this was the first time I'd been to his place, I felt relaxed, at home. When he sat next to me, I rested my head on his chest and sighed. As soon as I shut them, my eyes flew open, "How's the baby?" I demanded. "What happened?"

He pulled me back to his chest. "She's fine. She's doing good. She's home."

I felt the rhythmic thumping of his heart.

"Maybe we can go by Brenda's later today. I'd like to see her. See both of them."

"Maya?"

I sat up and looked at him. I didn't like his tone. "What's wrong?" I felt tears brimming in my eyes. I didn't think I could take anymore bad news.

"I owe you an apology."

I relaxed and curled against his chest again. If I were a cat, I'd purr. "No, you don't," I said.

"Yeah, I do."

The beating of his heart was like a mantra. I felt the tension easing from my body, my breath deepening with each inhalation and exhalation.

"I overreacted about your gift for Brenda. That's between the two of you. It wasn't my place to accept it or reject it."

I sat up and looked at Tony. It took a big man to admit when he was wrong. His remarks confirmed that what I thought I knew about him was really true. I rubbed my hand along the side of his face. I wondered if he realized how attractive he was. "You're right," I said. "On one hand, you did overreact." He nodded. "But on the other hand, you were right. Sometimes, people need something money can't buy."

"That's all I was saying."

I told him about my decision to volunteer at the North Avenue Project.

"That's great."

"But what?" I asked.

"Not to be possessive but if you're working sixty, seventy hours a week then volunteering at the North Avenue Project, what about me? I want some of your time, too."

I hugged him to my chest. He looked and sounded just like the little boy I hoped I'd have an opportunity to parent with him one day. "I won't be working those kinds of hours for awhile." Who knows? Maybe never. I told him about James Caplin and being fired from Musikiwa. When I saw his blood pressure start to rise, I made him promise not to do anything. There was no reason for him to jeopardize his job for something that was over and done with. I hadn't worked for James Caplin very long but I had developed the skill set I'd hoped to learn from him. I had figured out how to turn lemons into lemonade.

"Wow," he said. "So, what are you going to do?" he asked.

I shrugged and told him I wasn't sure. And for the first time in my adult life, it felt okay not being sure. I was financially solvent. Thank goodness. So, for a good while I wouldn't feel pressured to make a decision because I needed money to pay the mortgage. I had time to figure it all out.

"Did you like your job?"

I looked at him the way the young man at Starbucks

had looked at me a few days ago. I don't know if I ever really asked myself that question. During the months before graduation, Narcisco had been the most impressive company to offer me a position. Their executive training program was touted as one of the best in the business, so I accepted their offer.

I was good at my job. But I would be good at whatever I set my mind to. I wasn't being vain. I was being realistic. I liked being challenged. I enjoyed making a difference. But did I really enjoy the work? I wasn't sure.

"Sounds like you're in a great position," he said.

He was right.

"And if you need help with anything, I'm here for you. Just ask, okay?"

I would.

"Want a beer?" he asked. "I'm making chili for lunch."

I shook my head. "That's not all though," I said. "That's what's been happening on the job front."

Tony walked back from the refrigerator and lifted me from the couch. He wrapped his arms around me. "I'm sorry, babe," he said. "I'm *so* sorry."

I rubbed my finger along the vein that pulsed across his forehead. He looked so serious. "For what? What do you have to be sorry about?"

"That so much has been going on in your life over the past few days and I wasn't there to support you. To put my arms around you. To offer you a shoulder to cry on, if that's what you needed. To kick James Caplin's ass ..."

Tears sprang to my eyes. I put my finger to his lips to silence him. That was the nicest thing a man had ever said to me.

"That'll never happen again. Hear me?"

I nodded.

"I hope you never have to go through any crap like all this again."

"From your mouth to God's ears," I repeated an

*Surrender to Love*

expression one of my Jewish co-workers used to say all the time.

"I can't promise that you won't." He held me arms length away from him so that he could look into my eyes. "But I can promise you, you'll never have to go through it alone. Whatever the future brings, I'll be by your side as long as you'll have me."

When he pulled me back to his chest I knew that the words he'd spoken were true.

"So what else?" he asked.

I told him about my meeting with Cousin Lottie and the things I'd learned about my mother. "Now, I really wish I would have a chance to meet her. She sounds like a real character." He chuckled. "But I would have had her eating out of my hands,"

"Maybe so," I said. If anyone could have won my mother over, it would have been Tony. Then I told him about meeting my father.

"I can't wait to meet him," he said.

"I can't wait for him to meet you, too."

# Chapter 52 — Tony

I let myself into Maya's condo with the set of keys she had given me. Though we lived less than ten miles apart, it was becoming a hassle living in two separate places. Though I had a duplicate set of all my basics, toothbrush, a real razor, not those plastic things she used to shave under her arms, shaving cream, deodorant, socks, underwear and spare uniform at her place, and she had done the same at mine, invariably there was something one of us wanted that we hadn't thought to pack up and bring. In the past three months, Maya and I hadn't spent a night apart. We'd be in bed talking to one another on the phone and it would seem silly that we weren't together. So, either I'd pack up and go to her place or she'd pack up and come to mine. We were at the point that neither of us slept well when we weren't lying next to one another. I *was* pussy-whipped but it was more than that. Our relationship was a lot more than that.

I stood in the middle of her living room and listened. I followed the sound of her humming into the master bathroom. As I stood in the doorway watching her, I felt that familiar stirring in my groin. Her back was turned to me. She wore a sheer white cotton night gown, the outline of her underwear visible underneath. I knew when she turned around her breasts would be straining against the fabric and her nipples would harden when she saw me. As she did for me, I turned her on by just walking into the room. That encouraged me to spend even more time in the gym making sure I continued to look good for my woman. And she felt the same way. She'd joined the gym, too. It was great working out together. Or sometimes we'd go jogging along the lake. We'd both bought roller blades and would sometimes skate all the way to Evanston.

She kneeled in front of the oversized bathtub, singing softly to baby Deanna as she bathed her in a plastic baby tub she'd place inside the big tub. Maya had insisted on taking the baby for the weekend to give Brenda a much needed break. My baby sister had taken to motherhood like a duck takes to water but even the best mommy deserves some time to herself. She was a mom, but she was also a beautiful young woman in the prime of her life. She needed to get out there and explore who and what she wanted to do with her life beyond mothering my niece. Hopefully, she'd find someone else to share her life with, maybe have more kids, if that's what she and her future husband wanted.

And Maya was a natural with babies. Though I was sorry for the pain it caused her, I was happy she hadn't had a baby with another man. Though I'm sure she left out some of the detail, she gave me the highlights on her relationship with Deuce. I had promised her I'd be cool when it came to her former boss, James Caplin, but I couldn't make the same promise when it came to her former boyfriend.

I couldn't guarantee if I ever saw him I wouldn't kick his ass. I knew Maya was a grown woman but the man was wrong. He took advantage of her when she was in a vulnerable place. But I was the wrong person to pass judgment. No exaggeration, I would kill anyone who messed with one of my girls; my niece, Deanna, my sister, Brenda, and especially my woman, Maya. But all that drama was behind her now. When she had a kid, it would be mine. And we'd be first-time parents together. And I was sure that's the direction our relationship was heading, a permanent, lifelong commitment.

The more time I spent with her, the more things I loved about her. She told me what her mother used to say about her, and her moms was right. Maya was twice as smart as she was pretty and the girl was damned fine, so that was saying a lot. I read the business plan she'd written for the North Avenue Project. She was spot on. Just because it was a nonprofit didn't mean it wasn't a business. It needed a clearly defined strategic and tactical execution plan. She was taking the organization in a much bigger direction than Dean and Allison ever imagined, but I knew he would approve and Allison was on board. She'd given notice to her employer that she wasn't coming back from her leave of absence. It had become permanent.

And she made me feel like I wanted to be a better person. I'd been accepted at the University of Illinois so I was going to school part time to finish my degree. I loved being back in school. My fears that I'd be the oldest person in class were completely unfounded. Sometimes I was the senior statesman, but it was cool. In fact, if I were a different kind of man I'd have all the young, hot coochie a brother could handle. But most of the time there were other folks in class who had passed the thirty-year marker.

*Surrender to Love*

In one of my classes, the oldest student was seventy-eight, a black man. He hadn't learned to read until he was sixty-three. I had never really thought about the issues of illiteracy before, but he hipped me to the fact that more people than you realized couldn't read and write. They developed coping strategies to make it through the day, but it was a tough life. I took my hat off to the brother.

Once he'd learned to read he wanted to keep it going. He was aiming for a PhD. He said he wasn't sure which would come first, the degree or the grave, but as long as he was ticking he was going to keep on kicking. That gave me motivation to keep going. Maya was the only person with whom I'd shared this but I was leaning toward going for a Masters degree in Social Work. I really enjoyed the work I was doing with the kids at the North Avenue Project. I wanted to be qualified to do more.

"Hey there," I said to Maya.

When she turned around and looked up at me I wanted to fall down on one knee and ask her to marry me right then and there. No doubt, this was the woman I wanted to share my life with. But I wanted to do this right. Make it special.

"Hey babe," she said. My niece kicked her legs in the water and gurgled.

I knelt at the tub beside the two of them and poked her in the tummy. "You love your Uncle Tony?" I asked in a high pitched voice. "You love your Uncle Tony?" The baby giggled and gurgled.

"Are you going to ask me that question?"

I poked Maya in her stomach. In the same voice I asked her, "You love your big Tony? You love your big Tony?"

The three of us giggled. Maya nodded. "Yes, I do. I love my big Tony."

After Maya put Deanna to bed in the portable crib she kept in her bedroom we sat down to a dinner of Thai noodles.

"I love this stuff," she said. She dug into the carton for more. "I think I'm addicted."

Though we took turns cooking, we still ate out or bought take-out once or twice a week. I loved sharing the places I had discovered over the years and being introduced to the places that had been her spots. I really loved this thing she did every other week or so. She called it new and different day. It made dinner exciting. She would cook something she'd never made for us before and she'd go all out. Not just prepare the food, but create the entire ambience that went along with it.

If it was a Japanese dish we'd sit on the floor; if it was Ethiopian we'd eat with our fingers. She had the perfect plate or bowl or cup for whatever we were having. But like she said she wasn't hurting anybody. One time she'd prepared this Indian meal but before we ate she did a belly dance for me, costume and all. We ended up having *aloo jeera* and *seekh kebabs* at two o'clock in the morning. She should have known she couldn't move like that in front of a brother and think he would still have eating dinner on his mind.

"I finished the new business plan. Will you take a look? Be brutal, okay?"

I nodded. In addition to the work she was doing with the North Avenue Project she wanted to start a for profit company. "I don't want to let all the stuff I've learned from these white boys go to waste," she'd told me when we talked about it. I loved that. She really valued my opinion. She didn't always incorporate the suggestions I made, but I knew she took them into consideration. She wasn't just giving me lip service, trying to appease my ego.

I think a lot of sisters don't realize how much a man needs to be respected in a relationship, especially a black man. If he ain't getting respected at home, it's like the relationship is built on sand. It's going to shift around. It's never going to have a stable foundation.

And without that, it's inevitable — it's going to fall. A lot of men were messing around outside their primary relationship, not for the sex, but because the other woman made them feel appreciated, respected. Then again, some of them like her ex, Deuce, were just dogs, out-an-out low down asshole.

"Come here," I said when she was done eating. Since we'd been together she'd gained about ten pounds and it looked good on her. "We've got a good thing, don't we?"

She kissed me lightly on the lips. "It's better than good," she said. "We've got a great thing."

I agreed. We snuggled together on the couch. I turned on the game and she buried her nose in a book. The girl loved to read.

"Want to go to Delano's tomorrow night?" she asked me.

She had become quite the house-head since we'd been together. One time, we bumped into Monica. I knew it was just a matter of time before that happened. Even though I'd never taken Monica there, there weren't that many spots in Chicago that catered to house. The two of them were cool. I knew they would be. Monica and I had a good thing, for what it was, while it lasted, but we both knew it had run its course. And Maya knew that she was my girl. The babe had my nose open. And I wanted it to stay that way.

# Chapter 53 – Maya

When Tony and I walked into Brenda's living room, as usual she was asleep on the sofa with baby Deanna snoozing on her chest. Tony gently picked up the baby. If I didn't know her history, I would have never guessed her entry into the world had been so rocky. Her weight was right where it should be at six months. And she was a really happy baby. She knew that she was wanted and loved. And she had a group of adults whose mission in life was to make sure she knew *all* things were possible. She could chose options from an entire universe of opportunity.

Baby Deanna repositioned herself against Tony's chest without waking. Brenda's eyes fluttered open. "Was I asleep?"

*Surrender to Love*

"Not just sleeping," Tony said, "Mouth open, drool running, snoring-sleeping."

"Shut up." Brenda reached for the baby but Tony handed her to me.

"Hi, beautiful," I said. Deanna Antonia opened her eyes and kicked her feet. Brenda had put her on the outfit I'd bought for her to wear today. It was a blast shopping for baby clothes. I didn't tell anyone, except Deanna, and I knew she would keep my secret, I broke my own rule and paid full price for the outfit she was wearing. But I couldn't resist buying her first Roberto Cavalli outfit.

"Everybody in the family loves you," Tony said as he watched me and the baby.

I loved this little girl. I wanted to be the adult Deanna turned to when she didn't want to share something with her mom or she needed a second opinion. And Brenda had become like the little sister I'd always wanted. Though I would never overstep my boundaries, I knew *she* was the mother, I made sure to let Brenda know that she was not a *single* parent. She might be a mother without a husband, but the raising of baby Deanna didn't fall on her shoulders alone.

I had shed more than a few tears for my mother. It must have been so hard for her to carry the weight of raising a child all alone, especially when there was no need for her to. My father would have done more. He wanted to do more. Maybe, not in the way my mother would have scripted it, but in the way he could have, in a way that could ease the burden on her.

"You did good this time." Brenda winked at her brother. "Finally," she added.

"What are you guys talking about?" I asked.

"None of your business," she said. "Let me get my coat."

We both chuckled as she walked out of the room. She had shared quite a bit of information about Tony's dating history that had been none of my business. I knew Tony had better taste than she gave him credit for when she described some of the women he'd kicked it with. I liked it that they all sounded smart and successful. He wasn't kidding when he said he wanted an independent woman. But one thing Brenda said that was right on point, however, was that none of them had been the right woman for her brother. That was my role. And I planned to play it.

Even though it had only been six months since I'd left Musikiwa International, it felt like a lifetime. I was thankful for the experiences, and I meant *all* of the experiences, I'd had throughout my career there, but getting fired had been a blessing in disguise. If I'd still been working the schedule I had worked since entering the work force, there's no way Tony and I would be at the place that we were in our relationship.

There was such a thing as quality time, a relationship needed a significant quantity of time. There were certain things you only learned about a person through prolonged interaction. What were they like when they were sick? Or scared? Or stressed? Did they believe in God? How did that belief manifest itself in their life? Did their actions match up with their words? Anyone could be on their best behavior when the two of you were on holiday, what about the day-to-day?

I didn't share my new found insight with Donna, but I *had* figured out where I'd been making my mistake in previous relationships. It had nothing to do with not picking a man with the right pedigree. It had nothing to do with his job or how much money he made or his astrological sign, though Lillian swore the reason she and Rick were so compatible was because she was a Libra and Rick was an Aries so, as Sun Signs, they shared a complementary element. She assured me, at least astrologically speaking, that Tony and I were a good pairing because he was a Leo and I was a Sagittarius.

And slowly but surely, without even trying, Tony was

winning her over. After our first double date, she conceded that he was intelligent, well-spoken and well-read. There weren't a lot of men who could hold their own in a debate with Rick on politics and world events but Tony was one of them. That's what really cinched it for Ms. Lillian. Whenever the four of us got together, as soon as the first opportunity presented itself, Rick and Tony would be sequestered somewhere debating the meaning of some event. In Lillian's mind, if Tony was Rick's intellectual equal, then he could be a member of the club.

Of course, they weren't deep all the time. Sometimes when we thought they were off solving the problems of the world, they were actually watching the sports channel on cable. None of us, not even Donna who had an answer for everything, could figure out why men's interactions eventually had to include a ball. Football, basketball, baseball, golf, pool ...

"Or if they're not playing with a ball or watching other men playing with one, they're grabbing at their balls," added Lillian.

"Or trying to get you to suck them," said Donna.

"Too much information," said Lillian. We all laughed.

And I'd figured something out. I hadn't goofed up because I had selected the wrong *type* of man. Donna was right on that account. My problem was that I hadn't given myself enough time, or permission, to really get to know the person with whom I was involved. It takes time to get out of the relationship in your *head* and *be* in the relationship you're actually in. I may not have come to the table with preconceived notions of my wedding day, but I did have a lot of crap I needed to wade through. Everybody does. Though I knew I sounded like Lillian when she'd decided Rick was the man she wanted to marry, I thanked God every day that with Tony, reality was better than the fantasy.

"You ready for all this?" I asked Tony as we stood in Brenda's living room waiting for her to retrieve her and Deanna's coats.

He nodded. "Are you?"

"You'll be by my side, right?"

"As long as you'll have me."

# Chapter 54 – Maya

Ground had already been broken at the site for the new and improved North Avenue Project. Tony, Allison and I wore hard hats as we dug our shovels into the ground and lifted large piles of dirt. Light bulbs flashed and cameras clicked as James Caplin, representing Musikiwa International, handed the three of us an oversized check made out for three hundred and fifty thousand dollars.

Donna told me Carol had been let go. Position redundancies were the reason given. James continued his streak as wonder boy. He'd won major kudos from the leadership team in Japan for his commitment to support community efforts like the North Avenue Project. They felt he was the kind of executive the company needed — tough enough to deliver record profits while compassionate enough to care for the disenfranchised. The announcement of his promotion to Chief Executive Officer and Chairman of the Board would be coming out any day. I'd warned him that I'd saved the tape recording of our little encounter. And if I ever heard, even a rumor of his inappropriate behavior towards another woman, copies of the tape would go to the Japanese management team as well as the U.S. media.

So, good for him. He'd been able to leverage his screw up into another success. I still owned stock in the company, so I had a vested interest in Musikiwa's continued success. And as an added bonus, Musikiwa International had pledged to become the first client in the corporation I'd started. With the public school system failing so many students, it only made sense that entrepreneurs like me would step in and fill the gap while making a profit.

I was still getting my *Black Enterprise* magazine cover, this time in the issue on "People Making a Difference." My old mentor, Zoë Mitchell, would appear on the cover of the corporate power brokers issue. She had entered a small and exclusive club: African-American, female CEOs of Fortune 500 companies. I had a lunch meeting scheduled with her next week. It would be great catching up with her and sharing how the tidbit of advice she'd given me so long ago had positively impacted my life.

My hairstylist, Gustave, told me I'd earned a lifetime supply of free trims and deep conditioners when I asked him to do my hair for the cover shot. He said he could raise his prices even higher with that type of publicity. Though Latimer women tended not to turn gray, I wondered if his generosity would include free color if the time came. Probably not but I could afford to pay whatever he charged. My investments were really paying off.

Inside what was already being referred to as the old

building, balloons and streamers decorated the interior. I watched Cousin Lottie bring two saucers of cake and ice cream to Tony and my father. The two of them had hit it off like Tiger Woods and golf. I think Tony was becoming the son he'd never had and my father, Sonny Cleo Washington, was the father-figure Tony wanted in his life. Though Tony was the most together brother with whom I had ever been involved, even he had a hole in his soul in the shape of his father. My dad was helping fill it.

Lottie seemed happy, too. She had quit her job at the hotel and worked full time at the North Avenue Project, keeping the place clean and cooking. When the day care center opened, I told her she would have to hire a small staff since we planned to cook all the food on premises. And that was more than one person could manage, even a country girl from Jericho, Alabama.

"Ain't no mistake a girl can make that I haven't made," I heard her tell one of the pregnant girls. "But I'm living proof you ain't never too old to start fresh." She was a real inspiration.

"I can hardly believe all of this is really happening," said Allison. "A new housing development with subsidized apartments, a day care center and a full-time counselor."

"My mother always said God's plans for us are bigger than the plans we can imagine for ourselves."

"Your mother was a smart woman," my father said when he and Tony walked over to join us. "Crazy as hell but smart." We chuckled. I had finally learned that it was okay to laugh at my mother's foibles without feeling I was betraying her.

"And the center's gonna have a real gym, right?" asked one of the boys.

Allison poked her finger in his chest. "And parenting and relationship classes."

"Dean would be so proud of all this," Brenda said

when she joined our little group. Tony pulled her to him. She rested against him, his arm around her shoulder. "I hate it that he's not here."

"Without him, none of this would have ever happened," said Allison. "He's a part of it. He's here with us."

Brenda and Allison hugged one another, each a bit overcome with emotion.

"You sure you don't mind leaving UPS?" Brenda asked Tony when she pulled herself together.

"I can deliver packages or I can impact lives." Tony held up his hands as though he were weighing something on a scale. "What do you think?"

I'd been able to leverage contributions from a number of other major companies after Musikiwa's generous donation. We had enough to fund Tony's position as a full time counselor as well all the other improvements. No one had to know the history behind Musikiwa's largesse.

"Shut up," said Brenda.

"Besides, I'd do almost anything to get your lazy butt back to work," he teased. "I got to get some type of return on that college education I helped pay for."

Brenda slapped her brother on the arm. "Shut up."

"My hats off to you," said Allison to Brenda. "Being director of a day care center is no joke."

"Who you telling?" she asked. "The stack of paperwork I have to fill out for the state is about an inch thick." She kissed baby Deanna on the forehead. "But this way I get to work and keep an eye on my baby-girl just like my mom was able to do with me."

I didn't understand the look that passed between Tony and Brenda but he seemed to get it. Every family has its own special dynamics that only the members understand. And sometimes even they don't.

"Thank you, guys," Allison said to Tony and me. "Thanks for everything."

"We're just doing our part," I said.

Tony squeezed my hand. "Have I told you how proud I am of you?"

"Only about a hundred times but don't let that stop you."

He smiled at me. "Have I ever told you that I would very much like to marry you?"

I turned away from him to hide the tears that sprung up in my eyes and saw my father watching me. He smiled and gave the thumbs-up signal. He knew what Tony was about to do. When I turned back to face him, Tony dropped to one knee. A hush fell over the room as everyone watched us.

"Maya Marie Latimer, I'd be honored if you would become my wife."

I pulled him up from the floor and wrapped my arms around his neck.

"Anthony James Jackson, I'd be honored for you to be my husband."

He took a black velvet box from his pocket. The most beautiful two-carat emerald cut diamond engagement ring sparkled inside. I held out the third finger of my left hand. When he slipped the ring on, the room erupted in applause.

"I helped him pick it," Brenda whispered to Lillian. She looked at the ring and gave Brenda a high-five. She held one of the twins while Rick held the other one. The boys reached for Deanna. They were already protective of her. Brenda had gotten her wish ahead of schedule. Deanna had other kids with whom she could grow up.

"You did good, girl," said Lillian, who'd taken Brenda under her wing. She said Brenda reminded her of herself when she was that age. Lillian winked at me. I winked back.

Donna and Bradley raised their plastic champagne flutes filled with sparkling grape juice and nodded in my direction. They had decided to give things another try and seemed really happy. Neither wanted to start over. They still loved each other. I raised my glass in salute to them. I wanted Tony and I to start hanging out with them a little more, but they were caught up in one another, getting reacquainted. Good for them. Whenever they were ready to expand the circle, we would be there for them.

As I looked around the room I felt blessed. The only person missing was my mother but I felt her presence. I knew she was here with me. I knew she was proud of me. She knew her baby-girl had done good.

# Reading Group Guide

# Synopsis

# Surrender to Love

Maya Latimer is a woman with all the trappings of success. She has the dream job. She lives in the dream zip code. She is even blessed with two dream girlfriends who have her back through thick and thin. The only aspect of her life that always turns from dream to nightmare is her relationships with men.

After another devastating break-up, Maya swears off men until she meets Tony Jackson, the UPS delivery man servicing the swanky downtown office building where she works. Tony is the epitome of a good brother. Not only he is tall, dark and handsome, he has a good heart and a strong value system. Though Tony's pedigree doesn't match the credentials of the men Maya normally dates, she succumbs to Tony's charm. A series of dating missteps, however, leaves her track record of failed relationships in tact.

With Tony out of the picture, Maya commits to her

job with renewed zest. But for the first time in her career, work is not going well. When she refuses to give in to her new boss's inappropriate advances, Maya experiences another first. She's fired.

With all aspects of her life spinning out of control, a series of emotional events leads to a surprising revelation; Maya is more upset about her break-up with Tony than the loss of her position. With effort, Maya learns to move beyond her fears and ill conceived romantic notions until she allows herself to surrender to love.

# Discussion Questions

1. What are the key themes of the book? What message do you think the author is trying to convey to the reader? In what ways do you agree or disagree with the author's view?

2. Do the characters seem real and believable? Can you relate to their predicaments? To what extent do they remind you of yourself or someone you know?

3. How did each of the major characters evolve over time? How have you evolved in your own ability to surrender to love? What was the most difficult part of your journey? What has been your most surprising discovery? What prevents you from being able to surrender?

4. Were Maya and Tony evenly yoked? What makes a couple compatible? What are the qualities you seek in life partner?

5. Has the institution of marriage become defunct? Do you want to get married? Why or why not? If married, how has reality of marriage compared to your pre-marriage notions of how it would be?

6. How did Maya's relationship with her girlfriends change when Tony entered her life? Does the way you interact with your girlfriends change when you have a man in your life? Should it?

7. Did certain parts of the book make you uncomfortable? If so, why did you feel that way? Did this lead to a new awareness about some part of your life?

8. Would you like to follow the journey of the characters you've met in Surrender to Love? Their stories continue in Joy Comes in the Morning, available early spring 2008.

Maya and Tony's story continues in:

*Joy Comes in the Morning*

available early spring 2008.

Find it at www.amazon.com or
your local book seller.

CONTACT INFO:

www.deniserwilliams.com

deniserwilliams@entouch.net